TOTAL TIMEPASS

TOTAL TIMEPASS

A Light-Hearted Commentary on Indian Life

NARAYAN KUMAR

NU VOICE
PRESS

First published by NU VOICE PRESS 2025
An imprint of Hubhawks Pvt. Ltd
www.nuvoicepress.com

The characters and events portrayed in this book are fictitious. Any similarity to real persons, living or dead, is coincidental and not intended by the author.

ISBN: 978-81-990481-0-2

Printed at

Published by: Nu Voice Press

To my special friends Gayatri Vathsan, Venu Gopal Nair and Subramani Sarode who give me support, sustenance and the joy of their company

And to the unstoppable wind beneath my wings, Dipika Narayan

Contents

Prologue

Timepass: *noun (Indian English) - the action of spending time doing something, especially something that has no aim or is not very useful.*

It will not be a surprise if you end up finding this book useful. Stranger things have happened.

You hold in your hands a series of personal snippets, light sketches of city life in India as well as semi-rural shenanigans, thanks to my second home in the Nilgiri mountains.

You'll find confident, broad-stroke assertions about India as a whole in the manner of an untrained, casual observer with no self-restraint or self-doubt. Any topic is fair game.

To my open-mouthed astonishment, these snippets—when originally published as posts on LinkedIn—won me a good following and brand consultancy projects even though none of them specifically contained shop talk. No one knows how the world really works.

I have since credited myself with talent. A rare and well-honed talent in shooting my mouth off on random topics and somehow land profitable projects in return. If you disagree and think this book is trash, all you need to know is a refund is out of the question.

1

Home

Naming India

WHATEVER HAPPENED TO Gopal and Gowri, Ramesh and Rekha? Where did Vinod and Vasanti, Praveen and Priya go?

Have you noticed no one names their child with once-popular names any more?

There are no new Premas and Padmas today. Or Sanjivs and Sunils. We left them behind in the 90s.

Along with the Ashoks and Anjalis, Anils and Anuradhas.

Gone—alas!—are Sanjay and Shobha, Mohan and Mythili.

Even Andhra, once famous for classics like D.S.S.V.K.M. Rao, has moved on.

Geet(h)a and Seet(h)a? Vanished. Ramesh, Suresh, Mahesh? Forget it.

It all changed perhaps with Maneka Gandhi's extraordinary publication, *The Book of Hindu Names* which listed thousands of Sanskrit options with their meanings.

And with it came the habit of giving our children exotic names. Thus were born Kamna and Kanav, Mitali and Manav, Niharika and Nehal.

As also the brave new world of Anusha and Ahaan, Hamsika and Hriday, Mahima and Maahir.

With the popularity of the blockbuster *DDLJ* came a spate of new Simrans all over India.

The endearing batting genius, Sachin Tendulkar, spawned a million Sachins.

The ultimate movie villain in the 70s ensured no one named their son Pran, an otherwise lovely name. I still don't hear it in 2025.

Aptronyms, common in the West, were names of people who unconsciously pursued jobs and interests that matched their names. Psychiatrist, Jules Angst. CEO of Starbucks, Brady Brewer. Famous poet, Willam Wordsworth. Inventor of the toilet, Thomas Crapper.

India skipped aptronyms because we didn't know what anyone's name meant. It was just an identifying sound.

Kerala took it to another level. Parents grabbed the first letters of their own names and joined them to form a new name. Vinod and Nilima, for instance, named their newborn Vinil.

Next door in Tamil Nadu, Churchill, Einstein, Marx, Stalin, Lincoln, Washington and Newton came alive in earnest.

For all of India, Google offered nice sounds with or without mythology: Abolee and Angrish, Dhruvin, Adhideb and Arisha.

Srabbana and Chatura, Suprit and Alikhya thrived. While Hardik, Dikshit, Shitlesh, Anal and Sukhdeep caused mirth in US colleges.

The *-ansh* ending for boys had its run: Devansh, Meransh, Mivansh, Reyansh, Rudransh, Saransh, Sreyansh...

A class IV attendance register today features names that teachers never had for themselves: Ipshita, Kian, Mitesh, Shubhodayan, Sirisha, Sukhada, Yuvaan…

It's all exciting, spearmint fresh. With a competitive edge though.

New India wants the world to recognise that its next child is someone special. Someone unique. Not another generic Pradeep or Priya.

The nation is breaking into a sweat to give its new generation an advantageous start. To see them off the blocks. To set them apart. With a memorable sound.

And thusly a shiny new India is being born in front of our eyes—every mellifluous second.

Enjoy.

* * * * *

Indian Uncles

There was a time when every family had an Uncle who offered advice. It was your mother's brother. Or your father's cousin. Or a family friend. Or just an Indian-style 'Uncle' by being a certain age.

An Uncle gave you expert guidance and explained the ways of the world.

Since you only knew your classroom, your neighbour's house, the playground, an occasional cinema or circus and your own house, an Uncle dropped by to broaden your world.

He sipped your mother's coffee and called out your local Chief Minister as being very clever. Depending on his smirk or smile you figured out if clever meant scheming and badass or wise and resourceful.

If you liked an Uncle, you could tell him things. About that little ache in your tummy maybe. He became a doctor. "Tell me everything you ate from morning till now." He instructed your mother to "give him *ajwain* water right away."

If you returned with your cricket bat after play, an Uncle on the swing in your verandah said, "Do you know how Gavaskar used to practise as a boy?" He was a cricket coach too.

A literary Uncle told you of early birds getting the worm. A witty Uncle pointed out the flaw: but look what happened to the early worm.

A musical Uncle impressed you by connecting a popular film song to a classical raga.

A memorable Uncle once told us about his Air Force life. He was in grudging praise of the enemy's hi-tech aircraft—the powerful, US-supplied Sabre jets. I will never forget his face-down palm darting about this way and that, now high, now low. Yet, he said, we won!

An Uncle was influential. That's why your mother appealed to him. "Please tell him to study. He doesn't listen to us."

The best Uncles were the ones who took you out for a snack or an ice-cream or a movie.

The very best did all of the above in a single outing. You built a temple for them in your mind.

Sadly, you can't be an Uncle today. Try saying, "Look at the eastern sky tonight and scan for a big question mark. That's the Great Bear aka *Saptharishi*."

Before you lean back smugly at your own remarkable pronouncement, the 15-year-old twat in front of you will check his phone and tell you, "It's actually in the northern sky, Uncle." Punctured, you will quietly consider taking to drink.

Yet, the good news is Uncles are back—not in your living room but online.

Platforms like LinkedIn and Quora are natural homing zones. Because Uncles know everything, they tell us what's really going on in Bangladesh, how to win at Olympics and what to say in interviews.

Life nurturing advice is back, big time.

For extra guidance, Aunties have joined in with a photo attached to clarify they aren't Uncles. A heady mix of new ideas and plain old bullshit. And our world is vibrant once again. How do we know all this for a fact?

Because your Narayan Uncle just said so.

* * * * *

How families say 'I love you'

If you're in your 40s or older, your parents probably never said, "I love you" to you as a child. Or to each other within your earshot. In whatever language you spoke at home.

When I was five, I never sketched a stick figure of my father and scribbled "Bestest Dad in the World". He wouldn't have known what to make of it either.

None of my brothers told me, "You are the best kid brother anyone could have." I never hugged them tight and said, "I love you, bro."

Some emotions were easier to express. One of my brothers clearly conveyed to me that if I so much as touched his freshly ironed white shirt let alone wore it for my school cricket match, he would, as the first step, break my hands and legs and, as the second, kill me.

After an underwhelming report card of mine, my father thundered, "You'll be grazing buffaloes for a living."

Clearly, expressing emotions wasn't the problem.

The problem was—expressing love.

In the days long before today's miscellany of heart emojis, what was the language of love? How did those folks convey love?

In silence and awkward gestures. Which they bequeathed you so you also could pass on clumsiness as tradition.

Yet, for all that, you somehow felt their love. How?

Those folks of yesteryear did something clever. They *acted out* their love instead of talking.

A sis-in-law knitted a sweater because you were leaving for Delhi to study. An aunt made you *sabudana khichdi. A* brother bought Test match tickets *with* popcorn. An uncle took you to watch planes land.

The language of love was effort, not words.

In later life, you too came back from a hill station with wintergreen oil. It was a way of saying, "O beloved aunt of mine. This potion will magically rid you of your knee pain."

Of course, you couldn't talk like that, so you spoke of utilitarian benefits: its top quality, keen smell, tribal provenance, etc. A good aunt ignored your rubbish speech and saw your gift for what it was: love. That's why she looked at you like that.

Today, the tradition of silence is breaking.

More parents today are bequeathing a new language of openness and self expression. Folks say "I love you" to their kids. Heart emojis abound. I love it.

Western influence, wider exposure, whatever. For a bottled up generation, this is so freeing.

Love is still effort; it always will be. But it now has an accompanying language instead of an accompanying silence.

With today's words, a schoolboy me could have asked my father, "Why did you feel the urge to buy me costly, studded, custom-made, pure-leather cricket boots (with Blanco)?"

He'd have said, "It was my own love of cricket." Or, "Your mother said to." Or, "As the youngest, you were very special."

I would have known for sure. Instead of imagining intent, as I am now.

Love needn't be a guessing game played out in silence.

*****

Creativity at school

Creativity shows up early in life. A school kid whose nickname for a teacher is approved by the rest of the class is already starting life as an influencer.

Really good nicknames are not easy to create. To call an overweight fellow a 'Fatso' requires no creativity. It takes minimum observation and a bit of rudeness.

If you're talking about high quality nicknames, you are talking about high quality observation and high-quality rudeness.

Children have an innate ability to observe forthrightly without polite, social filters. They make connections that are not immediately obvious and state them bluntly. What else is creativity if not making unexpected connections?

We had this Sanskrit teacher who took a short cut to reach our school. We watched him from a window at the back of the class negotiating the marshy waste that separated the main road in the distance from our compound.

He could have used a proper road instead. But that would have added 15 minutes to the journey. Each morning, we saw the bare-chested, elderly man in his spotless white dhoti, clutching a cloth bag and making the epic commute.

He stood on a dirt mound, safe for the moment from the marshes. He scanned his immediate future and chose the next dirt mound that looked sturdy and also close by.

He jumped onto it. He surveyed again. He jumped again. In a varied dance each morning—the mounds and marshes were never in the same place every day—he took small jumps and reached school by slightly different routes.

With all the concentration involved, he never realised that there were a number of kids watching his progress from the class windows.

An anonymous kid—I wish I could recall his name and learn what he's up to today—came up with the perfect nickname for our Sanskrit teacher.

Armstrong.

There is something inherently funny about mentally connecting a cutting-edge, scientific product of NASA, the first man on the moon, with a humble, traditionally clad, cloth bag-holding professor of an ancient language. Just because both did the 'moonwalk' on a strange landscape with amazing similarity.

That's the kind of jump, lunar and otherwise, that a creative mind makes. You can do nothing but applaud.

In rare cases, such as this one, the nickname gets the full treatment. It gets handed over to posterity to be enshrined in the minds of future generations of kids. Armstrong, our Sanskrit teacher. Remember the name.

Sure, there is the poking fun aspect, the rudeness and the implicit putdown that come with nicknaming. In today's troubled and sensitive times, such acts will be considered thoughtless and in bad taste.

If you can ignore all that for a moment and see it for the superlative creative act that it actually is, you will know what it takes to be really observant, really spontaneous and really long lived.

Good, creative stuff is a refreshing, if not great, leap for mankind.

*****

We love 'homely'

Homely is a word Indians love. Homely food, homely stay, homely bride...

After my last schooling year, I got a part-time job and made friends with a much older Raj, who was a foodie and palmist.

"How's the food?" I asked him at the canteen.

He had just stuffed his face with searing hot *upma* and was now in torment. In sign language, he touched the tips of his forefinger and thumb to indicate quality. (No emojis then. We made real gestures.)

"Homely food," he said, calming down.

He meant non-commercial food, the kind made at home. To a school kid, it was insipid and boring. To him it was non-spicy, non-oily, tasty, safe.

Homely, as a word, also goes with hotels.

In a small, unfamiliar town like Jatni or Ranebennur, you want a homely place to stay.

This may mean anything from a 'clean room where they change the sheets daily' to 'a free Medimix soap and hot water, but it's fine if a tiny cockroach shows up in the washbasin.'

It also means affordable. Homely stays can never be expensive.

Homely, as a word, also goes with brides.

On that same hot *upma* afternoon long ago, Raj read my hand. "You'll get a homely wife," he predicted. There was that word again.

Either Raj knew only a handful of words or I had much to learn.

Homely wife? I thought of my aunts and older sisters of friends and figured out a composite. I decided a homely wife cooked well, stayed at home, read many books and wrote "How true!" along the margins of those books.

Tracking down the 'homely wife' continues to this day. Who exactly is she? The hunt is on at Quora:

Homely? There are a lot of women who don't want to work. There are a lot of women who are simple in dressing and manners.

The quest to define continues in matrimonial ads:

Hindu, 32, MBA, 10 lakh p.a, 178 cm, owns business, seeks a bubbly Tamil (non-Facebook user.)

I want a girl with no drinks. If she wants she can wear jeans in house but while stepping out of house she should give respect to our caste.

And here's one for the ages. A groom's profile, quoted verbatim, from a popular matrimonial site written to attract the homely kind, presumably.

I would love to be an amorevolous husband, being in a state of eunoia, making small moment a special one for my partner, creating an ambiance of cynefin with surprising petrichor.

Ye homely ones. Does this dude stand a chance with you? As a nation, we agree more or less what homely food and homely stay are. But a homely wife? Where do we even start?

*****

Be Indian, be frugal

If you're an Indian, you must be a frugal person. It's not about being a cheapskate, it's about getting value. Most of us do frugality very well. Instinctively.

Long ago, when my little son was having his asthmatic episodes, an elderly relative suggested we take him to a yoga institute.

She accompanied us to the institute and we met up with a senior instructor. He taught a few breathing exercises and recommended 'balloon practice' every day.

"Get a packet of balloons," he said. "Let him pick one for the day and blow it a few times. The next day, take out another balloon and blow it a few times. And so on for a few weeks."

It made sense. I could understand the need to build strength in the lungs and how 'balloon practice' might help.

The instructor turned away to talk to a colleague. My elderly relative leaned over and in a matter of fact tone whispered, "Why buy a whole packet of balloons? Can't he blow the same balloon every day?"

This is the frugality mindset at work. It isn't even about money at all. A packet of balloons costs nothing, so it's not really about the expense.

It's about wastage. It's about value. Why acquire more than necessary (and pay for it too)? Why not extract value from what's already there? That's how the frugal mindset thinks.

In the 80s and 90s, I've seen many an Indian family settling in the US getting a Toyota Corolla. Why? Because it did everything nicely while doing no one thing spectacularly.

Fuel consumption? Reasonable enough. Speed? Fast enough. Build? Safe enough. Space? Ample enough. And, the main thing, the price? Affordable enough. So, overall rating? Sensible enough.

Middle-class neighbourhoods like Vile Parle and Matunga in Mumbai have the best vegetable prices. The residents (or their frugality mindsets, to be exact) keep the prices in check. If someone charges more, they will go out of business.

I've come to notice that this mentality is also universal. People like Jeff Bezos moved with their family to the countryside to live simply and save costs in the early days, long before he turned Amazon into the Amazon we know today.

One of the richest men in the world, Warren Buffet, still lives in a relatively humble residence, not a palace.

I wonder if the reason so many top international companies hire Indians as their CEOs is because of our inbuilt frugality meter.

*****

When you turn 90

We celebrated a close relative turning 90 at our society's banquet hall. Folks from the Laughter Club, Senior Citizens' Club, neighbours, etc. gathered for banter and lunch.

One elderly lady, in her late 70s, asked for the mic to share her memories of the newly turned nonagenarian.

"When I came to this society some years ago and wondered about joining the Laughter Club," she said, pointing to the birthday boy next to her. "I met this handsome man who had this big laughter coming from deep within. Not everyone can laugh like that. He became my crush. I joined the Club."

With the applause that greeted her, she went on. "What if we both had been in our twenties? We could have made something happen between us. Who's to say, no?" More applause.

The birthday boy played along. Everyone looked at his wife seated next to him. She was in her eighties.

The speaker then addressed the wife, who in her younger days was well known for her striking beauty. "I'm not saying he would have fallen for me. I know Auntyji here was very much the Mala Sinha and I wouldn't have stood a chance. But I'm just saying. Happy birthday!"

Her brief speech ended. The applause was thunderous. No one had expected anything like this. Light, entertaining, fun.

Everyone looked at the wife. The grand old lady looked at the speaker and gestured with an imperial wave of the hand. "Take him!" she said.

The room lost it. It was minutes before the laughter and applause subsided.

A 70-ish person, an 80-ish person and a 90 year old had produced a memorable, light-hearted interlude out of nowhere. A dutiful, solemn occasion turned light and spontaneous. The smiles spread across the room in waves.

Just that morning, the birthday boy had told a few of us, his close ones, what it felt like, turning 90. "I don't know really," he said. "It just happened and I'm 90 now. Here I am."

And so, it will be with the rest of us. One day we will turn 40 or 50 or 60 or whatever. And we will be none the wiser how we got there. We will feel both bewilderment and acceptance at the rapid passage of time.

And quietly get on with the concerns of the moment—like ordering multigrain bread, remembering a relative's name, reporting a misused credit card, scouring the Netflix menu.

It would be extremely nice if we could do what the three wise people did at that gathering: Share a little joy with our well-wishers.

For all the ups and downs, rights and wrongs, routines and adventures, and God knows whatever else life is about, it's great to remind ourselves that humans can do that one special thing animals and plants can't.

Laugh.

* * * * *

The phone scam

I got scammed a few weeks ago—almost. Hoping it doesn't happen to you.

A recorded call said my line would be cut in a few hours for non-payment. Dial 9 for more information. I had an urgent call soon. I dialled 9.

The Wman said my phone number was being used to cheat people. He read out a mobile number and asked if it belonged to me or my family. No, it didn't.

Did I buy a SIM card from a particular shop recently? No. Could I visit a specific police station in the next hour to make a statement? No, not within the hour.

Could I put you on to the police line, he asked, to complete the formalities directly. I said sure.

A gruff voice came on the line. He verified my name, address, etc. and told me he could conduct the investigation right then if I was willing. I said, sure, let's get it done. He told me to come on Skype.

He spelt out that unknown number again and asked if it belonged to me. No, I said. It was bought in your name, he said.

Shit. Someone was misusing my identity and I had to clear my name now.

He showed me a part of his own room with a computer, documents, a walkie-talkie and a close-up of his badge hanging round his neck. It had a photo, a name, a Sub-Inspector designation and a registration number.

"What's your Aadhaar number, Mr Narayan? Can you send me the copy?"

I read out the number. Had I lost my card recently? No.

"Let me make a call to Delhi," he said. "Hang on." He called someone and this was the convincing bit—a voice answered him with the hiss of a walkie-talkie: "Yes. Come in. Over."

The man gave him my Aadhaar number. The other guy's crackling voice repeated the number. "Give me a few minutes. Over."

He got back saying the person with this card number was wanted in a public scam case. "I'm sending you the documents. Over and out." The policeman now spoke to me.

"Narayan," he said sternly, dropping the Mr. "Are you hiding something from me?" He sent me documents about a criminal behind bars who had defrauded people. Was I part of that group? Was I anti-national? He had proof!

Wha-at? Where the hell was this going? He said he had proof I had false savings accounts in SBI and ICICI to dupe people. I said no. "Think carefully before replying," he warned.

"Then where is your account? Which bank? Tell me the truth!" he demanded.

That instant, my stupidity vanished. I saw how he had led me with a mixture of assistance, fear and a walkie-talkie, to get me to—almost—share my bank details with him.

"Sure," I said cheerfully. "I'll come to the station and give you the details."

"Narayan!"

"Yes?"

"My superior will arrest you instantly. Let's talk now."

I told him to fuck off and cut the call. That was close. I have conducted workshops all my life and I will tell you this. He was a well trained pro. He was not winging it; he was working from a script.

Moral of the story: Don't dial 9.

* * * * *

City lights

Some of the stuff learnt in early years are impossible to unlearn. Even though I grew up in a metro city, the street lights were not that powerful then. At night, you could see the stars if you stayed up late, after the city went to sleep.

It felt nice to be in the dark. By ten or eleven, the sky put on a dazzling show.

My big brother showed me the leading lights. There was the Great Bear or *Saptarishi* over there in question mark form. If you wanted to show off, you called it Ursa Major.

Follow the path of the last two in the line and six times their apparent distance away was the Pole Star or *Dhruv*. To show off, you called it Polaris.

He gave me a name for the three stars in a curious, oblique line: Orion's Belt. Overhead was the Milky Way. Rising above the horizon, the constellation of Virgo. Cassiopeia. The Dog Star, Sirius. Venus, the brightest thing in the sky after the moon…

It was difficult to say what exactly fascinated me about the skies, but I sat up late over months and years as a kid.

Then life happened. Powerful sodium vapour lights in cities happened. A profusion of high rise buildings happened. And my move to an even bigger metro happened. And the skies were forgotten.

Years later, with wife and young son in tow, I lugged an oversized telescope with tripod to smaller towns like Udaipur to find clear, unpolluted skies.

In the simpler world of those times, a security guy at the airport asked me what it was that I was carrying. Not knowing the Hindi word for telescope, I made up one on the spot. "It's a… it's a… a Doordarshan." Not understanding my gibberish, he asked me directly and plainly if it was a gun. I said no and he let me pass. We saw the rings of Saturn for the first time on that trip.

Decades later still, lying on the sands of the Sahara in southern Morocco, it was a staggering sight to see a clear night sky filled with frighteningly beautiful stars. About a million of them.

I peered nervously to see if I could make sense of the jumble. To my delight, I recognised Orion's unmistakable slant. Ursa Major was there. So were Cassiopeia and Canis Major. Aries. Polaris. Jupiter. The Milky Way, of course. And the cluster of Pleiades… and more.

Moving my head this way and that, spurred by an old memory kicking in with confidence, I remembered them all! For someone who forgot the names of people met two weeks ago, this recall was remarkable.

My old friends of the night were still up there, making their safe passage through the night. Just as before. How reassuring, somehow!

For all the life changes I'd gone through, Orion and the gang were sticking to their regular routine. For all the tumult I'd been through on earth, it was clockwork in the heavens.

Nothing had changed, really. All was in order.

You want perspective? Look up at the humongous balls of fire, billions of miles away from us and from each other, marching to a plan that is way beyond our pay grade to comprehend.

Pitted against that vastness, you gain a realistic measure of the petty weight of your own concerns and troubles on a speck called earth.

What's that, you say? You can't see the stars for the city lights?

Head for the hills, if not the Sahara.

And watch the greatest show on earth.

*****

Family criticism

Family criticism is a universal thing. In India, you just turn up the intensity. In South India, you turn the knob fully clockwise.

The main weapon in family criticism always was comparison.

"Look at your cousin, same genes. But she cleans her room twice a day!"

"We are a family of doctors. Except you."

"Your brother always topped the class."

"Ashish next door, your friend—first rank in Maths!"

The Maths Obsession. Taken to the next level in South India. Long ago, my good friend showed his report card to his dad.

"96 per cent in Maths," said my friend, soft and deadpan. You would never let on you were satisfied.

His dad verified it, also deadpan. "The remaining 4 per cent vanished where?" he enquired. As a rule, your parents, uncles, older brothers or sisters all gunned for what you missed, not what you got.

So that "you can improve." Other families compared you to dead people. They held as shining example the late grandfather who studied under a street lamp and joined the civil service.

Many families claimed these exemplars of studiousness as their legacy. The spaces beneath street lamps must have once been densely crowded.

In the 90s, a TV ad for Cadbury's—*Pappu Pass Ho Gaya* (Pappu Has Passed)—showed a whole colony of people sharing chocolates on the joyous occasion.

Kids in South India wondered what the fuss was about. How come they were getting chastised for scoring 95% while their siblings in the North were jiving in the streets for *just passing?*

I once heard an 8 year old girl confront her mother. "Why do you say bad things when I do so well?" And the mother snapped back. "So that you don't think too much of yourself."

A daily drip of criticism was meant to prevent swollen heads in later life but ended up making kids think *less* of themselves. And unable to handle praise.

When a European client lauded me at a product launch for the "brilliant campaign for our third year in India," I deftly stonewalled. "It's nothing. Third time lucky, haha."

He looked at me puzzled. "If not for your two earlier campaigns, there would be no third year now." People like Dale Carnegie made pots of money selling self-help books for a good reason.

Today's middle-class, South or North, is strong, confident and bullish.

Young guns like Gukesh Dommaraju wouldn't have reached lofty heights in the chess world if his parents had told him, "not to think too much of yourself" and wilt at criticism.

But I sometimes wonder.

What happens if you are a regular, unspectacular kid who, by sheer bad luck, lives next door to a Gukesh?

Will your mother resist the temptation to say, "That boy next door has made his parents feel so proud, no?"

It's the comparison weapon again. Just when you are chomping a tasty, hot pakoda on a rainy day, it turns to ashen *vibhuti* in the mouth.

And your guilt-laden inside teeters like a toppled pawn.

* * * * *

2

Village

Ganesh and Eashwar

ONCE IN A while, a friendship happens out of the blue. A year ago, my nephew and I were driving in the Nilgiris when I took a hasty curve and ran over a rock that had slid onto the road. The front left wheel was torn to shreds.

We were stranded. No phone signal. Stuck near the edge of the road with no room to change the tyre.

A car approached and stopped. Two men got out. The younger man folded his spotless dhoti to knee level so that he could examine the nether regions of my SUV. To a city-bred lout like me, spontaneous assistance from strangers was unusual and touching.

Ganesh, the older man, got talking. They were big shots. Each owned 50 acres of land.

Eashwar, currently sprawled beneath my car, was the village headman who, among other things, settled divorce cases as a judge. He was also a SAP expert, educated in Germany with work experience in the UK.

It began to drizzle. A blood sucking leech wedged itself between Eashwar's toes. The working space was too restrictive. He gave up after toiling on slushy ground for half an hour.

They gave us their numbers and left, promising to send a local mechanic.

Everything went to plan. The mechanic arrived in his tempo truck with heavy-duty implements. In minutes we were homeward bound.

It was only natural to call Ganesh and Eashwar home for lunch. They had great advice on how we could improve our environs with saplings, flowers and herbs.

Over subsequent visits, we exchanged gifts like shirts, Bombay sweets and Kolhapuri chappals from our side and a local vegetable called *chowchow*, *rajma* and eucalyptus oil from theirs. My wife and me were guests of honour at Ganesh's daughter's wedding.

Under their guidance, a lush garden is magically springing up around our house. We installed electric fencing, cleared the slopes off lantana and ringed the perimeter with bamboo shoots.

We patiently await the growth of lime, guava, pomegranate, peach, plum and green apple trees. Unthinkable for a regular urban couple!

Even more unthinkable is the fact that I keep thinking of dahlias and poinsettias. Tea tree saplings and night queens. Sage and oregano. I pretend I'm a local rich man with huge hectares to tend. I give myself landowner airs.

Even within our tiny space in the hills which we visit a few times a year, a surprising new life has opened up. Full of trees and flowering plants.

Think about it. What are the odds? A city slick gets a flat tyre on a mountain road, meets a local judge who is also a techie with international exposure, sees his knees covered in copious mud and ends up making a couple of new friends who help his garden grow?

Dumb luck, I know.

"What's this I'm hearing about you," a friend in Mumbai said. "You've become a gentleman farmer, I believe?" I told him that the farmer bit was true. It marked an exciting new turn in my life.

The gentleman bit, of course, could be argued.

*****

John Sullivan invents the Nilgiris

In school, I became friends with a boy who collected words the way others collected stamps or matchbox labels.

Following him, I came across 'gorse' and added it to my collection. It sounded good. But what did it mean? The heavy-duty, family Chambers dictionary—yes, children, these were the days before Google—told me it meant 'furze'.

Furze? What was furze now? Turned the pages of Chambers to check out furze.

It said 'furze' meant 'whin'. What? Turned more pages. It said 'whin' meant 'gorse.'

A circular definition if ever there was one.

Three lovely words in my collection and clueless about any, especially 'gorse', my starting point. Life was perplexing and fully curved. You ended up where you started.

(Turned out 'gorse' meant a shrub or bush, but that understanding came years later.)

Decades later, I saw a new word in *The Guide to the Blue Mountains* by D.Venugopal. A proper noun.

John Sullivan.

He was the British collector from the nearby plains of Coimbatore who literally invented the Nilgiris (including Ooty, its famous lake and tea estates) with a sheer climb over 6 days losing 25 men.

His first stop was at Kotagiri, where I now had a second home. I knew villagers here who still adored him and celebrated his birthday.

The guide book (also a fantastic history book) said Sullivan's original house still stood, refurbished, in Kotagiri.

It was now a records museum of a bygone era and well maintained. The guide gave its location, its history and its "neatly-finished wooden staircase."

Sullivan's Bungalow was a gorgeous building. I took out my Nikon to frame it against a blue sky and fluffy, white clouds.

I heard a booming voice from behind. "Are you interested in the building or the man?"

I turned around. Past the manicured grass and the compound wall, on the second floor balcony of an adjacent house, an elderly man in a sweater was sipping tea.

"Both," I said. And he invited me over, just like that. "Come and meet me. I'll tell you about John Sullivan."

My internal BS meter warned me: *Beware, self-appointed local guide approaching.* Every famous place was full of them. I had my book. I didn't need a guide. "I have to rush," I told him. "Maybe later some time."

He gave me his number. "Dharmalingam is my name."

I went back to my exposure settings, relieved. As I clicked the shutter button, something else too clicked in my head. I whirled around to see if the man was still there. He was, sipping tea and watching me. "Dharmalingam Venugopal?" I asked. He smiled. "Yes, that's correct."

This man was the author of the very book that brought me here! *The Guide to the Blue Mountains* by Dharmalingam Venugopal. It was my turn to be friendly and civil, if not sheepish.

"Your book is in my car," I said, pointing down the road. "I'm here because of it."

So, the book gave me John Sullivan and his bungalow. The bungalow gave me the man in the sweater. And the man in the sweater gave me back the book with his autograph in it.

I knew a pattern when I saw one. It was the same gorse-furze-whin thing all over again. Delightful.

Everything comes round full circle.

*****

Balu markets himself

Want a great lesson in sales and marketing? Forget Kotler, Jobs and Iacocca. Find a real world, Indian teacher. You'll learn better.

Balu is the watchman of the combined, adjacent properties of a few of us friends in the Nilgiri hills. He is also a versatile fixer of everything from water pipes to local politicians.

While he gets a monthly salary for his regular work, he thinks up fresh ideas as side hustle extras. Like a good salesperson, he focuses on the benefit, tells a story and builds urgency.

A while ago, Balu came to me and said that while fencing my whole area would be expensive, I could fence a part of it. Sure, that made sense.

It would provide safety to the parking area and protect the flower beds from stray cattle. That was the key benefit. Reasonable, scaled down, not easily dismissed.

He showed me phone videos of bison in the area clearing 5-foot high gates without breaking into a sweat. By sharing these videos, he silently primed me on the need for adequate, high fencing.

"Besides," he said, "it is a good idea to safeguard the parking area, night and day, from predatory bears and wild elephants. Everyone knows from the newspapers, some elephants had destroyed the nearby tea estate the previous year."

That was the story. The bison videos caught the imagination. Vivid imagery of wild animals going berserk on one's land took hold.

A relative of his was visiting the nearby town shortly with a tempo-truck that would be returning empty.

"If we tell him to, he can pick up the fencing posts the coming week and deliver them to us for practically no transportation costs," Balu said.

That was the built-in urgency with savings thrown in.

Who could resist? I told him to work on a quote and let me know. Balu reached for his shirt pocket and pulled out a piece of paper with a ready, hand-written estimate.

The fence got done and I'm proud of it too.

Never mind that there were enough passages in the slopes for stray cattle to get through and still eat our plants.

Never mind that an occasional bison did visit the place at night. Never mind that no one had seen a bear or elephant on our land in years and that protection from them was illusory.

But the Balu Fence stands fiercely tall. It is somehow a comforting thing.

He is already talking of securing the place with three tall, wooden, lockable gates at strategic points along the fencing. He will explain in person when we meet next. And I'm waiting to hear his compelling story as it will turn out to be.

In the hands of a good salesman, we are willing to be moulded.

As Balu (and Jobs) will tell you.

*****

Birds and squirrels

Periodically, you want to expand your skills. Stretch. Try out a why-not. To add to my regular travel shoots, I decided to explore bird photography.

My place in the Nilgiris was home to lapwings, bee eaters, bulbuls, robins, pipits, barbets, flycatchers, wood pigeons, spotted doves, babblers and the elusive Malabar Hornbills.

No dearth of subject matter. Felt like a good move.

"Can your camera handle low light?" asked a fellow pro in Mumbai. Yes, it could. "Do you have a long lens?" Yes, I did. "Do you have a bird feeder?" No, I had a cook and a gardener, but no one to feed birds.

He called me an ass and sent me to Amazon. I bought 2 plastic bird feeders. I hung them from the deck roof.

In the bedroom adjoining the deck, I set up my tripod and camera. All ready to capture birds partaking birdseed from bird feeders. Exciting. Would I ensnare a rare hornbill? Would it feature on NatGeo's cover?

No birds came. The leaflet said birds would take time to find the feeders. It advised patience.

In the manner of the old, calming Sanskrit mantra of the Buddhists:

Om mani padme hum.

Breathe deeply now.

It took 3 days before the first visitor came down the roof: A squirrel.

It sniffed at the feeder. It invited its friends. Hanging upside down, they chewed through the hard plastic. The seeds spilled to the ground. They gorged everything.

"Don't cow down," emailed my friend. Squirrels are evil. Buy new feeders.

He sent me a book. *Outwitting Squirrels: 101 Cunning Stratagems to Reduce Dramatically the Egregious Misappropriation of Seed from Your Bird Feeder by Squirrels.*

I found the long-playing record stratagem interesting and workable. Link three long-playing records (remember those from way back then?) with a plastic clothesline through their centre holes, keeping an 8-inch gap between them.

Now suspend the linked LPs, it advised, from the roof and attach the feeder at the bottom. Squirrels would fear to step on wobbly, unsteady records to reach the food.

This project was getting more complex than expected. I no longer thought of birds. I dreamt of squirrels.

But the crazy contraption did its job beautifully. The LPs stymied the stupid squirrels. They stopped short. No food. They scooted. My new feeders hung safe and tall. Victory!

But—no birds came. They flew to their regular Nilgiri joints instead of my newly opened McDonald's for Birds.

I didn't fire a shot. It was impossible to do bird photography without birds. That night, an angry thunderstorm smashed everything to the ground. The new feeders broke open. The squirrels returned to feast. Damn.

Thus ended my photo adventure with nothing to show for it. You can't fight a grumpy universe that denies you birds and hands out squirrels and storms.

You can only wait it out. For luck will turn. Ambitions will renew. The universe will behave. Until then...

Om mani padme hum. Breathe deeply now.

*****

Hariharan

Celebrity culture is big in India. It borders on worship. I personally know this.

I sometimes get mistaken for the singer-celebrity Hariharan in places as far apart as Salem and Ellora. Owing to my long hair and who knows what else.

It gets over in a few minutes usually.

In the Nilgiris where I have a home, it was different. I attended the wedding of the village big shot's daughter. I was touched by Ganesh's earlier gift of a large sack of rajma and *chowchow* from his estate. I wanted to reciprocate by being there for his big occasion.

(It was a different matter that we ate *chowchow* daily for a whole month in Mumbai.)

When we reached the hall, an excited village *pujari* spotted me. "Here comes Hariharan," he announced to the crowds. "I swear on Shiva!"

Ganesh's brother welcomed us at the entrance. His wife gushed. "I enjoy all your songs."

They led us down the centre passage of a high-ceilinged hall with a thousand people in it. A live band played Tamil songs. Two bedecked old ladies in the front row were summarily asked to vacate their plastic chairs for the chief guests. We sat down.

Groups of people now came at me in waves for selfies.

Courteous, excited and in a queue. The video guys on stage turned around and trained their lights on me and the fans.

A young man lovingly chided me for looking older than he imagined. The lead singer went off key, nervous because of me. I smiled kindly to calm him down.

In the dining hall, a tilak-wearing man saw me from afar. His eyes bugged out and flew off their sockets. He rapidly criss-crossed the long rows of tables separating us, dodging servers with silver buckets, and reached me, hands folded.

"Hariji," was all he said. He dived under the table to touch my shoe. Dazed, I couldn't think of anything less vacuous than asking if he was from the girl's side or the groom's.

Fan worship was real. Strangers freely gave love and appreciation. And the effect was incredibly heady. I could get used to this.

People were inclusive. Everyone invited my wife to come into frame—even though, presumably, the real star's wife wasn't a celebrity herself.

Imposter syndrome was real. The fear of being found out and rocks being chucked at me persisted.

The real dread: what if someone asked me to sing a famous Tamil or Malayalam song?

"Took care of that," Ganesh explained later. "Told them you were a gentleman. Fine with selfies and chitchat but hated being asked to sing. Don't cross the line, I warned them!"

Mischievous man, pulling a trick on his own people, including his own brother. His brother shook hands. "You made us happy."

I waved an upbeat presidential goodbye to all. With no stone pelted, we left. Laughing kids ran behind our car.

My mugshot, as my friends and colleagues will tell you, bears no resemblance to Hariharan. But try telling them that in Kotagiri. Or in Kodaikanal, Salem and Ellora. They'll laugh at you.

Even if you swore on Shiva.

*****

How to build a village road

Useless projects. All of us go through them. In college, to pass a subject called Community Service, we were sent forth to build a rural road.

Fifty of us reached a village, armed with digging implements. The villagers told us they were already happy and didn't need a road.

We said, "We cannot accept that. We have come a long way for this. Please understand." Besides, there were marks at stake.

After whispered discussion, one of them led us to a clearing some way off.

"Start from there," said the man, pointing to the jungle scrubland. He made a sweep of the hand, pointing to more scrubland. "And end it there."

His message was clear: we were free to make a road as long as it was far away and didn't disturb them.

Our supervisors and boys broke into smiles. Great. Exciting. Time for action! I silently swore I would play no part.

Everyone started work under the fierce sun. I hung about in the shade. Everyone grabbed a shovel or a pick-axe. I chose a non-violent metal receptacle—a small, shallow pan to hold sand or gravel.

When supervisors came along, I placed the pan on my head to suggest I was transporting material. As a variation, I inspected it for cracks and defects. They left me alone.

I did not dig, shovel, flatten, carry, clear or help anyone in any way. I loitered, and at the first opportunity, sat down in the shade. This went on for six days.

The dismal project had its joyful moments, though.

The morning bath was exhilarating. The rapid, cold rush of water from a field pump was not only bracing but also strong enough to fell a full grown ox.

Evenings were spent with friends on a culvert by the highway. Legs swinging freely, we watched the dusk settling in. We noted with interest that the sound of a truck approaching us was different from a truck leaving us.

The night sky had millions of more stars than I knew. I identified all that my brother had taught me—Orion, Great Bear, Pleiades, Canis Major, etc. Venus in the low horizon and the faintly reddish Mars overhead. Good stuff.

Whoever was making the food—a student, a supervisor or a local cook, who knew?—was a genius. I looked forward to mealtimes. Relaxing in the shade for hours on end made you hungry.

By the end of the week, the road to nowhere was ready. A village elder was persuaded to give away awards to the Best Pickaxe Wielder, Best Shovel Expert, etc. There was no award for the Best Dodger.

Once home, my father asked me what exactly I'd done. My mother said, "He has toiled in a village and returned tired and charred. Let him rest." I crashed into the pillows and slept for 18 straight hours.

Even pointless projects teach life skills.

Of how to avoid the limelight, stay invisible, enjoy the good parts and never get caught.

* * * * *

What to gift a Panchayat head

Gifting is awkward business. We all know that one toaster or tea set, gifted at a wedding, gets endlessly recycled through many other weddings.

It's difficult to know what to gift a family member. It is nearly impossible if you have a friend, like I do, who is a village panchayat head.

He is not the 'village head' as you probably imagine him to be. He studied SAP in Germany and worked in the UK for two years. He came back to his family home a decade ago and became the headman of his village.

He wears a golden Rolex, a spotless dhoti and colourful shirts. He sports a *tikka* on his forehead. Before he drives off in his Scorpio, he reaches for his RayBan glasses.

He grows carrots, *chowchow* and tea over 50 acres of land. He speaks fluent English, Kannada and Tamil.

What do you take for him from Mumbai?

The reverse is easier. A village head can gift you tribal cloths or handicrafts, varieties of tea, local snacks, eucalyptus oil or produce from his farm. Exotic!

The first time he gifted us, his farmhand came over and opened a cloth bag to show its contents. I dipped my hands in and came up with two *chowchows* (local vegetables that look like pears and taste like ridge gourds), one in each hand. As I thanked him, my friend laughed.

Take the bag, he said. Not just two *chowchows.* Are you trying to insult me or what? (It's a different story that my wife and I ate *chowchows* daily for a whole month in Mumbai.)

For my recent visit, I called and asked him directly. Did he want anything special from Mumbai?

He was thankfully one of those nice, uncomplicated people who gave you a direct answer instead of a coy, "Your friendship is good enough," which didn't make your job any easier. He told me to get him an accessory for his new Scorpio.

We scoured Amazon and chose an interesting little perfume dispenser in the form of an aeroplane. When we checked the delivered package, it had a few moving parts—a nose propeller, the plane itself, a base, a bottle of perfume, a little metal rod for God knew what, some screws and a few more items. Although we had other things in the hamper, like a tee for his son and Bombay halwa, this felt like a cute addition.

On reaching our Nilgiris home, we had second thoughts. This was a cheesy gift, we felt. What were we thinking when we chose a frivolous toy with propellers and metal rods for a grown man?

We gave him the gift bag. He instantly wanted to see what was inside. He picked up the dispenser package first as we squirmed.

"You are a magician!" he said, surprised and happy. "How did you know I was looking for just this exact thing?"

He explained in detail what the contents were without opening the package. And he was absolutely right! He mentioned two of his cousins who had the same thing and how he was planning to get it on Amazon but never got round to it.

Of all the gazillion things available on Amazon, it turned out that, somehow, we had hit upon the jackpot. Thus, restoring our faith in the universe to reward us when the intent is right.

Gifting, it appears, can be satisfying.

*****

Simp and sump

I need a water storage solution for my house in the Nilgiris. Balu, our watchman and general adviser, suggests I install a 'simp.'

A what? A simp. He points to a neighbour's house up the hill. "Like that one."

Does he mean a sump?

"Yes," he says. "Simp. You can say it like that also." By mutual consent, I keep saying 'sump' and he keeps saying 'simp.' We communicate.

Meanwhile, Kamlesh, the handyman, says the pressure pump coil has burnt out and advises buying a new pump. Any brand recommendation? He suggests 'Girloskar.'

You probably guessed—he meant Kirloskar. That's because you saw it in print. But hearing it as a spoken sound made no sense—until the package arrived.

It's the same thing with my electrician in Mumbai. When he bends low from his high stool to ask me for a 'paana', he means a spanner.

Why do people hear 'sump', 'Kirloskar' and 'spanner' but end up saying 'simp', 'Girloskar' and 'paana'? What's going on here?

Sounds from another language don't always fit neatly into our set of familiar sounds. So, we twist them to fit.

This is not new. About 2,700 years before Kamlesh was born, the ancient Greeks knew about Chandragupta Maurya in faraway India, but spoke of him as Sandrakottos. That was their style.

In the 16th century, when the Arabs heard the Turks say *kaveh*, they called it *qawa*. The Dutch heard the Arabs but called it *koffie*. We now call it coffee. The British heard Thanjavur but said Tanjore. They heard Alappuzha but said Alleppey.

It wasn't just foreigners. We did it too.

The great Ashoka said that his moral law was applicable even across the Narmada to the Chodas and Panidas (Cholas and Pandyas). The Greeks would have called them Pandae and Charmae (Pandyas and Cheras).

Of course, some sounds were simple and travelled well. The Canton Chinese said cha. The Portuguese had no trouble saying cha. Neither did the English. It remains cha universally.

But the Min Chinese said té for the same thing. The Dutch picked up the sound and gave it to the English. It remains tea to this day.

On the other hand, some words were near-impossible to say in the vernacular.

Cab drivers in Mumbai were taught by driving school instructors to say 'race' for the foot pedal that makes it go faster. 'Accelerator' was hard to say, so it got replaced.

Total replacement is an exception. The more common rule is to take foreign sounds and reduce them to natural, familiar sounds.

It's why Malayalis find it simpler to say 'simble' for 'simple.'

In a popular, apocryphal story, two Tamil actors plan to go for lunch."Let's check out this new restaurant called Bobby Ganesan," says one.

When they reach the place, the other guy exclaims, "You dog! It's Barbecue Nation, da."

You say it your way, I say it my way. Balu approves.

*****

Honey Shiva

There are experts and then there are other experts. The first kind are those who offer knowledge and talk a good game. And the others are the ones who actually solve the problem.

It cuts across domains.

A while ago, a swarm of bees took over the roof of my homestay in the Nilgiris. They entered the master bedroom. They stung my caretaker.

As owners sitting in faraway Mumbai, we had no clue what to do.

It was a repeat of what happened a year ago when we were there at the homestay. I asked around for help then. Many local 'experts' increased my knowledge without solving the problem.

I learnt that fire could smoke out bees. But questions like how much fire and who'd apply it went unaddressed.

I learnt that a local tribe—the Irulas—were experts at smoking out bees. Where could you find an Irula? No one knew.

I learnt more stuff. That wooden houses faced this problem because of little gaps in the roofing girders. I learnt that kerosene worked. And a lot else.

No solution in sight, though.

Until the gardener called a couple of local boys over. They climbed a ladder, shoved their spindly hands into a crevice and tossed out a hive.

Simple as that.

Great news, the local pundits enthused. They opined that bees never returned to the same place once tossed out.

Wrong again. The bees had returned now.

This time, I went to my own tribe—a Facebook group of Nilgiri residents. Within the hour, someone gave me the number of Shiva.

Shiva was so effective, I was told, that he preferred everyone save his name on their phones as Honey Shiva, not plain Shiva.

I did nothing of the kind. I saved it as Bee Man Shiva. He listened to me carefully and said he'd take care of it.

Our caretaker later told me that Shiva came with a box. He plucked out the queen bee from the hive in the woodwork and clipped its wings. He placed it in the open box.

Every bee in the vicinity plunged in and settled there. He walked into our bedroom and the portico with the open box, inviting all bees to get in and stay put. They obliged.

He closed the box with finality… and buzzed off. Job done. Not before advising us about minor gaps in the woodwork that should be covered by putty.

We gladly paid via Google Pay. The guests came in next day, had a wonderful time without meeting a single bee.

And me? I edited his name on my phone as a mark of respect to a true expert.

Honey Shiva, I typed.

*****

Kannan the naturalist

At our homestay in the Nilgiris, a guest asked us if there was a naturalist who could take them around. Naturalist? In this wilderness?

We made enquiries and discovered Kannan from the nearby town of Kotagiri. In smart camouflage clothes, he offered us bird watching trips, tribal lifestyle exposure and mountain treks.

For decades I'd trained myself to move slow and sure on even surfaces, so I declined the trekking bit. We took the car instead for a nature trip at dawn.

He knew every tree. He identified palm-sized birds in flight from within the moving car. He plucked the sweetest guavas. He made us see the same roads and hillsides in a new light.

"Take note of that hill," he pointed across the valley. "For five years, I've been seeing a herd of elephants there. Must be the jackfruit trees… keep an eye for them when you pass this way."

I had blindly driven past this spot at least a hundred times. He showed us parakeets and flycatchers. He told bear stories. He led us through dark woods.

What was that tiny bird over there? A green bee-eater. What was the tree I was leaning on? Fig. When was the best time to see the fabulous hornbills? November to March. What was that green thing on that low branch?

"My cap," he said.

On the tea slopes, a huge bison raised its head to observe us. We backed off. Kannan pointed to a tall tree and said that the hornbills came there to roost every November.

Precious information. My house was close by.

At a roadside tea stall, a standard cup of tea tasted spectacular. Even though the steam fogged up my glasses, I drank in the view—a world far removed from my Mumbai flat's view.

As a child of the mountains, Kannan read a lot on environmental issues. He wrote articles in newspapers on preserving the habitat.

After a chastening IT stint in Bengaluru with high BP and diabetes, the local boy had returned home. For a healthier lifestyle. And better earnings, at that.

I'd read about ancient, prehistoric caves somewhere close by. I asked Kannan if he knew. He said that he had petitioned the government to close them down for visitors.

Why? To protect them from tourism vandals, who defaced the precious walls for fun.

The sun was climbing. It was time for Kannan to meet his next set of clients, a younger lot in track suits, eager for serious trekking. And time for us to leave.

We left, convinced. From that day on, Kannan became our homestay's go-to guy for any guest who asked for a naturalist. We recommended him without hesitation especially after spending an eventful day like that with him.

It reminded me of my school days when we had to write an essay on our day at the beach or zoo or somewhere special.

All of us ended our essays in the same way. We went home tired but happy.

*****

Vinay the cook

Balu is the watchman of our little community of six households in the Nilgiris. He is also our Odd Job Man.

He knows everyone. He does everything.

He clears the undergrowth. He fixes fuses. He beckons a carpenter. He runs errands with the local government. He tells you which plants to grow. He pays your local taxes. He is supremely confident that you can't do without him.

On the other hand, my gifted cook Vinay is a one-trick pony. He cooks. Period. He doesn't even buy the groceries or do the cleaning up afterwards.

Who gets the groceries, then? Balu, of course. And who cleans the vessels? Balu's wife, Chitra.

It's a tenuous relationship between the two men. Balu speaks only Tamil, Vinay only Hindi. Somehow, they communicate.

A sharp difference of opinion surfaced recently. It was about a roving shepherd nearby.

We ourselves had noticed this shepherd before. He was a strikingly tall man. Unlike a villager, he wore jeans, a tee and a baseball cap. He held a crook and tended his cows and goats.

We wondered if he was really an urban dropout from Bengaluru living a life of pared down basics in search of nirvana. Because of his lanky frame, long hair and pointy beard, we named him Jesus. The Shepherd of the Mountains.

Balu freely allowed Jesus to graze his cattle and goats in our estate. He said they helped get rid of unwanted plants and overgrowth.

Vinay objected. He disliked seeing strangers and beasts out of the kitchen window. The emotional score line was clear: Balu liked Jesus. Vinay disliked both Jesus and Balu.

Generalists like Balu get over-busy and spread themselves thin. With many odd jobs for many people, he kept messing up his grocery commitments. It was clear we needed a reliable replacement.

Specialists like Vinay have time to stay focussed and plot. Vinay found out that Jesus had a Scooty and spoke to him (in which language, we will never know) offering a steady side hustle for extra income. Jesus agreed to buy our groceries.

We reached the Nilgiris and a cheerful Vinay introduced us to Jesus—a quiet, dignified man—and we finalised him as our new groceries-procurer. The emotional score line pivoted.

Vinay now liked Jesus. Balu disliked both Jesus and Vinay. He argued that the security of the premises would be compromised by letting outsiders have free access to our property. Vinay dismissed it as total rubbish.

Specialists get their way in the end.

*****

3

Away

YouTube loves India

WE ENJOY OUR movies and songs. But we also want foreigners to enjoy them and tell us so. YouTubers from the US to Africa, Mexico to Korea have all hit upon the market formula: Praise India. Monetise.

They make reaction videos to Indian songs. And we go nuts. All of us—Bengalis, Telugus, Tamils, Marathis, Punjabis...

Our Stupid Reactions, a US channel, reacted to the movie song *Malhari*. "Ranveer! Incredible energy!" yelled Rick, the host. We rewarded him with one million views and pure emotion. An Indian viewer commented, "It melts my heart to see you embrace the beauty of Indian culture."

We gave 3 million views to the reaction video of Kaushiki Chakraborty's classical music. A Bengali commenter gave arbitrary information. "She's from Kolkata, the City of Joy."

Reacting to a Zakir Husain-Rakesh Chaurasia video, Rick, eyes closed, said he was transported to a world of butterflies and meadows. A commenter provided cultural context. "When Lord Krishna played the flute, animals went into a peaceful trance."

"Indian women are so beautiful!" gushed Jaby Koay on his channel, reacting to *Dola Re Dola*. Delighted and proud, Indians gave him a whopping 1.8 million views.

A commenter gushed back with obscure detail. "Aishwarya's ears were bleeding from the heavy earrings but she told no one until after the shoot."

The Korean Dost channel did a reaction video of the Tamil song *Arabic Kuthu* and sang along with it. We went berserk and gave it 6,12,000 views.

A joyous commenter wrote, "The way Hoon sings, it looks like he'll soon learn Tamil." We lose it when the world loves us.

When *Naatu Naatu* got the Oscar, the British Indian couple of Sureet and Stevie went ballistic. "Crazy dancing! Will watch it again and again!" Delirious with joy, Indians gave them 6,00,000 views and posted their comments sharing background detail and trivia.

"Jr NTR had a car accident but still dances with unbelievable speed."

"Telugu is a wonderful language with 56 longest alphabets."

Latinos Waleska and Efra reacted excitedly to the movie song *Pinga.* "Love the costumes, choreography, dancing… wow!" Returning the love, a commenter suggested a helpful next step to the Mexicans. "You should learn about Marathi culture."

There are hundreds of India-praising channels mushrooming. They supply praise from their couch. If stuck, they ask us.

Hey folks, what do you want us to react to next? From our regional corners, we holler back: Ram Charan, please. Shraddha Kapoor, please. Thalapathy Vijay, please. Shreya Ghoshal, please. Zakir Husain, please. Please, please.

Enjoying our art isn't enough. We want foreigners to chip in and stamp it as great.

So, they react. We like, subscribe and comment. We set in motion the never-ending cycle of us enjoying foreigners enjoying us. We want praise and a place in the world. They want views and a livelihood. We barter.

And everyone goes home happy.

* * * * *

Boarding gate

Mumbai International Airport is meant to be a silent airport. There are no announcements.

While waiting at our departure gate, we heard a lady's booming voice from a distance shouting a single word.

"Dubaiiii!"

In the dead of the night, the lady with the energetic voice was walking the long passages and making a non-microphonic, raw-power announcement.

The voice came closer, earth-shaking.

"Dubaiiii!"

She was at our gate. She was a surprisingly frail lady, collar bones showing, greying hair, bespectacled, a name card hanging around her neck… but what a stentorian voice!

It reminded me of Brad Pitt screaming at the fortress gates in the movie *Troy*: "Hector!!!" Loud, urgent, demanding action.

She had four assistants, all blue-uniformed men with normal voices. They asked us if anyone was headed for Dubai. That flight was leaving shortly and they were looking for a stray passenger.

Our gate was for passengers travelling to London but they were taking no chances.

They woke up sleeping passengers. It was instructive watching the expressions of people in deep sleep being woken up by a stranger asking a strange question, "Dubai?"

The lady and her group, unsuccessful, went away to other gates and her announcements got fainter and fainter.

In ten minutes, they were back at our gate.

"Dubaiiii!"

Everyone was wide awake now. Her sharp eyes spotted one guy opposite us who was (somehow) oblivious to her clarion call and remarkably in deep dreamland. An assistant shook him and popped the question, "Dubai?" And the man nodded yes!

Why a man bound for Dubai was sitting at a gate meant for London we will never know. How they missed him the first time around and what instinct brought the search team back to our gate we will never know.

But there he was, instantly alert, grabbing his backpack and already running. He was hustled in the right direction by a couple of assistants who took off with him shouting to unseen officials up ahead that he had been found.

I did notice that the passenger had bloodshot eyes. It may have been the late hour, a busy day or something imbibed.

I also noticed the Lady with the Stentorian Voice. She was looking at her noisy assistants running away in the distance. Expressionless, she looked like any of us who turned our phone on or laced our shoes, nothing special.

One more night and one more wayward passenger hunted down. Big deal. All in a day's work. Ho hum. In Frankfurt, Chicago or Sydney, if you fall asleep, you miss your flight. No lady with a powerful voice is going to save you.

But this is India where a huge miscellany of us with different backgrounds, exposure, livelihoods, education and whatnot, all occupy the same spaces and co-mingle. And we are required to look out for one another.

True, the so-called silent airport was shattered by a booming voice repeatedly. Equally, a traveller was rescued in time and sent packing to Dubaiiii.

* * * * *

The invisible tigers of Kanha

If you're into wild life holidays, you would have noticed a whole cottage industry that works to instil hope in you. Of an imminent tiger sighting.

We were in Kanha National Park in MP.

Of the 4 zones—Kisli, Mukki, Kanha and Sarhi—our hotel manager advised getting tickets for Kisli.

"Blindly book," said the manager. "How many tigers you want? See them all at Kisli." On the wall behind him, a tiger photo stared at us fiercely.

On the first safari, the guide showed us pug marks on the ground. Wow, we said. We saw spotted deer and big spiders. We took photos.

In the afternoon, the guide beamed. "Fresh tiger shit," he pointed. The implication was if recently vacated excrement was here, then the defecating beast should be close by. "Thrilling," we all agreed. We looked around us sharply.

On the second day, the forest officials at the gate recognised us. Other visitors, they said, saw not one but four tigers. Our hopes soared. "Try Mukki."

On the third morning, we saw little birds and more deer. We stopped taking photos.

At the tea shop near the gate, folks showed off their tiger videos. We saw footage of two tigers striding. Another showed a tiger still, posing for the camera.

We faked happiness for them. "Which zone?" Kanha, they said. We headed there for our last safari.

It rained.

Fat, ice-cold raindrops pummelled us. The overhead tarp was pulled out but the jeep was designed for maximum viewing pleasure, not protection. The rain came in at a slant and slapped us.

We rushed back to the entrance. End of trip.

The ticket office area was abuzz. Munna, the oldest tiger of Kanha, had been spotted—of all places—on the main road leading to the reserve.

Surprised drivers of parked cars watched the decrepit old animal, too weak to hunt, pick up a buffalo on the highway as easy lunch. They saw it drag the carcass into the tall jungle grass.

Even though we had proper tickets in our pocket, Munna put up a free show for drivers instead.

We later complained to our hotel manager who had strongly recommended Kisli. He smiled kindly. "You will see a tiger not when you're ready but when it is ready to see you." Very Zen.

For now, shivering and wet, we reached our car. Nearby, hiding in the jungle grass, a couple of tigers were no doubt watching our dreary exit. They raised their majestic paws to their majestic mouths—to stifle their majestic laughter at sods like us.

*****

Pakistan and Kohli

They are totally watchable. They run popular cricket channels on YouTube—from Pakistan. They speak their minds. They are raw and emotional. They raise their voices to blood vessel-bursting-levels to criticise their own cricket team.

While they have their own points of view, they are united in one thing: their adulation of Virat Kohli.

The co-host of Sawera Pasha's show, Syed Ali Imran, held his head in his hands at Virat's tantalising near-century. "Just 5 runs, he lamented, just 5 runs, *yaar*." He was also smiling because Virat had—yet again!—shown the world what an unparalleled chaser of the cricket ball he was.

So disappointed, and yet so happy, he admitted. King Kohli had no equal, he pronounced. All comparisons with anyone else (hint: Babar Azam) were a waste of time. The matter was once and for all settled.

Veteran sports journalist Waheed Khan waxed lyrical. If there was a crown given to batting second and guiding one's team to victory, it should sit atop Virat's head forever. "This guy is unbelievable," he said.

On Rizwan Haider's channel, the co-hosts gushed over Virat's consistency and were scathing about their own team's inability to follow suit. Did they even watch the King and pick up a lesson or two on how to plan a chase? They doubted it.

The ex-cricketer Salman Butt, perhaps aware of talking up a rival country and appearing unpatriotic, declared that Kohli did not belong to India alone. He belonged to the entire sporting world. Having cleared the issue, he went on to praise the computer that Kohli had for a brain.

It wasn't the hosts alone who were singing the praises. Regular people on the streets of Lahore and Karachi joined the hymn.

There was only one king, they said. King Kohli.

It was unreserved praise. This was especially ironic given that the head honcho of the Pakistan Cricket Board had, just a few months ago, indiscreetly and publicly referred to India as a *dushman mulk* (enemy country). Yet, here they were, the general public gladly taking Kohli into their hearts.

Great sportsmen freely cross borders. A Federer, a Messi and… a Kohli.

My wife, uninterested in sport, dropped by. "Who were we playing?" New Zealand. "Were we winning?" Yes, I replied. Because of a crazy man called Virat Kohli.

She asked if I'd followed up with the Asian Paints people on the painting quote. I put my head in my hands—just like Syed Ali Imran across the border.

There are evidently two kinds of people in the world. Those who love Kohli.

And those who couldn't care less.

*****

Searching in Satara

Whether you are an atheist or a believer, you recognise a superior power above.

You obey it. You know it watches your every move. If you're lost, it will point you in the right direction. You call it by whatever name you wish.

Most of us know it as Google Maps. Our Eye in the Sky.

A year ago, we were on a road trip on NH 48 to the Nilgiris where we have some land. Nearing Satara, I felt the urge to visit a hydroponic farm on a whim.

In the year of the pandemic, we did an online hydroponics course. We learnt about growing stuff with only water, no soil—lettuce, carrots, spinach, basil, broccoli, cauliflower, etc. Could we try this out on our land?

As city folks, we hadn't grown anything beyond our own hair and nails. This felt new and exotic. The people behind the online course had told us about this demo farm of theirs in Satara and encouraged us to visit it when we could.

"Suddenly? Just like that?" said my wife, unwilling to get off NH 48.

"Where is your sense of adventure?" I said.

We made a call, got the address. The Eye in the Sky instructed us to skip the next flyover. At a teashop, a man in a purple shirt was sipping tea.

We entered a factory-type compound and stopped beside a car. I called Sachin, our contact. "We are here," I announced.

"I'm coming," he said. But he never came.

He called me this time. "Where are you?" he asked.

"Next to your blue Maruti Dzire," I said.

"What Maruti?" he inquired.

"Right next to the steps," I replied.

"What steps?" he repeated, puzzled.

Clearly, he was somewhere else. He sent me his location. It was 6 kilometres away.

"Just follow Google," he said, "and you won't get lost."

Really?

We now drove past the same teashop where the man in the purple shirt was still sipping his tea.

In 5 km, the blue line doubled back and ended in a familiar place: the teashop. The man in the purple shirt was now chewing a bun. End of route. End of my patience. I stopped.

"Google be damned," I hissed. "Hydroponics be damned. Let's get out of here. We are NH 48 people. We don't belong here."

"Where is your sense of adventure?" my wife asked. She was deeply into solving Satara now.

On its own, the Google arrow moved. It pointed to a new road. I drove slowly this time. In rural places, perhaps, Sky Daddy needed more time to compute. We crawled. On the screen a new left turn popped up. Aha! See?

Except there was no left turn.

There was a slight gap between two fields. A bicycle may have gotten through, not an SUV. Sachin called.

"Any landmarks? What are you seeing?"

"Sugarcane," I said.

Reading off the map, I told him that we were on Karkhana Road.

"No, no," he shouted. "You should be on Degaon Road!"

I braked. I breathed. I closed Google Maps.

I did what paleolithic people did to find stones. I stopped a passerby, a real human and asked him. He told me. And we reached Sachin's farm in three minutes flat.

O all ye good people, learn this. When your mighty Gods let you down, turn to your fellow mortals.

They often have the best answers.

*****

Xuangzang

My school text book called him Huein Tsang. It said he came to India and saw great things. It had a paragraph or two for us to manage the exams with.

Today, he is Xuangzang, the great Buddhist scholar.

He was a walker. He walked westwards for 500 miles because there were no Toyotas or Airbuses in 627 AD.

He sought the original Buddhist manuscripts because the Chinese translations were inaccurate. Those were in faraway India. No problem. Merely a few thousand miles more to go.

Since the regime forbade foreign travel, he hid during the day, walked at night. While bargaining for a horse in a border town, they arrested him. He escaped in the night.

Across the fierce Taklamakan desert, without Google maps, he picked his way among skeletons in the sand and horse droppings. A police chief shot arrows at him but later became a friend.

He lost his way often. He let his water cask slip. Precious liquid vanished into the sand. He rode four days without water. His horse disobeyed and went its own course. That somehow led to green pastures and a fresh water spring. Friendly villagers showed him the way ahead.

In the icy Pamir mountains, wearing double shoes and thick fur clothes, he slept in the snow. On the other side lay the bustling, international trading town of Samarkand, the Singapore of its day. He made friends and they showed him the newest Buddhist shrines.

He entered India from the north west. Highway robbers stole his possessions and money.

At Bodh Gaya, he saw the famous tree cut down. He noted that Buddhism was on the wane. Nearby monasteries were derelict. On a boat ride on the Ganga, bandits decided to offer him as human sacrifice to Durga. He accepted his fate and asked to pray.

A violent storm set in from nowhere. The bandits took it as a warning from above. Afraid and penitent, they set him free. Unaware of anything, Xuangzang opened his eyes and calmly asked, "Is it time now?"

People in the famed Nalanda university—among the greatest human institutions ever—heard of the foreign visitor and sent word for him.

It was the Harvard of its time. Admission was near impossible. "A hundred lectures went on in a day in different classrooms," noted the stupified Xuangzang.

The great Buddhist scholar Silabhadra took him under his wing. And he found all the manuscripts he came for. The Sanskrit originals—at last!

He spent six years there, studying and transcribing. He went back to China, twenty years after leaving it, with loads of valuable notes.

1400 years later, here we are. With better air conditioning, travel options and computer algorithms.

We still navigate random circumstances, good and bad. We still navigate other people, good and bad. And we still reach somewhere satisfying in the end.

We are all journeymen like Xuangzang. With varying degrees of what he had in abundance.

Luck.

*****

Beyond Mumbai, an ocean

It is in the nature of things that an ocean offers no firm footing.

The Arabian Sea, unlike the Sahara, takes no footprints. Whoever steps on it goes in it. And watches a Netflix movie of their whole life at 100x speed.

Yes. I'm deathly scared of water. I can't swim.

Last week, Uncle D called. "Let's go sailing. Wednesday, 4 pm. Wear a cap."

I agreed. Why?

Uncle D was 81 years old. He was a member of the prestigious Yacht Club. He owned a sailboat. He liked me. I computed that a person like that had no reason to drown me. But did I agree too fast?

That night, I dreamt of kind dolphins guiding me to safety.

My friend, Gayatri, messaged me. "Don't worry about sea monsters. What monsters? No monsters." I had strange friends.

They scared me about things I never considered.

High tide at the jetty. The boat bobbed wildly. Too risky. Doubts arose. Why do this? What was so wrong with my life on land that I had to visit the sea?

Dinesh, the boatman, gave me a life jacket with many buckles. It was bright orange. The orange was probably chosen to help the dolphins spot me easily from the blue-toned sameness of the deep.

Dinesh raised the sail. It caught the wind and swelled. We were off! Towards the deep blue yonder. No petrol. No battery. No AI. Just wind.

To overcome fear, I took charge. I tapped the boat. "What wood is this?" Uncle D said, "Fibreglass."

Ships of yore had wooden planks. The longest plank from bow to stern was called the 'devil.' To keep the ship safe, a diver went below to repair leaks while caught literally between the devil and the deep blue sea. Scary thought. I counted slowly to ten.

We picked up speed in strong winds. Pencil-length tassels tied to the steel ropes fluttered horizontally. "Telltales," Uncle D said. "They show the wind."

Like lipstick on a collar signalled adultery, telltales on a sailboat signalled wind direction. I smiled. Sailboats were not bad.

A bit of ocean rose above the rest of ocean, split into droplets and slammed me in the face. Salt on my lips. Seagulls sat on buoys. The mood lifted.

Dinesh loosened the ropes. "He's taking the wind out of the sails," Uncle D explained. "He knows his ropes," I added, enjoying the nautical banter. Where did the fear go now?

Dinesh expertly swung around the overhead sail arm without beheading us. The boat did a U-turn. We headed home.

I stood up. Hands on hip, I gazed at the city skyline nearing. The deck was wobbly. But I was Columbus. I was da Gama. I was Nelson. World domination! Land ahoy!

"Sir, please sit," said Dinesh.

We got off at the jetty. Two hours had flown by. I bade goodbye to both the Old Man and the Sea.

"When are you inviting me again?" I asked brazenly.

"You call me," he smiled and melted into the melée of tourists, touts, klaxons and chaos that was Mumbai. I drove home and messaged my friend:

You were right. The sea holds no monsters at all.

* * * * *

Sign language

Thamsanqa Jantjie. You don't know him. But you should. Jantjie was a sign language interpreter.

When foreign dignitaries visited Pretoria, Jantjie stood alongside and translated their speeches in sign language, live, on state television.

So far, so good. Except Jantjie did not know sign language.

Jantjie just moved his hands randomly during speeches. When experts analysed a phrase during a particular speech (later on), it meant:

3 words, first word. What does the box say? Ringdingding from the garden, SMS three thirteen fourteen now, now your left foot in, put your left foot out, do the hokey pokey.

Another phrase was translated as:

Hello, welcome so far. Well, cigarette join, bringing in different to you. A circle, I would like to pray this offering, basically, this is fun, all of this.

Basically, bilge.

Jantjie brazenly converted political speeches into nonsense. (Shouldn't be difficult, you say.I hear you.) Hired via a recruitment agency, he remained on government pay for five years.

He only knew 4 authentic signs: a two-finger salute to his forehead to signify 'greetings'; a circular motion with a finger to mean a 'circle'; a two-finger movement to his lips to mean 'smoking'; and a rapid opposing movement of fingers and thumb to mean 'blah-blah.' He mixed them up in various permutations with added random movements.

Complaints from folks hard of hearing literally fell on deaf ears. No one took action. Jantjie thrived.

During Nelson Mandela's memorial service, Jantjie stood next to Barack Obama, ready to go. Unlike the previous local telecasts, this one was beamed to millions around the world.

A lesser man would have said, "Pass" to a major gig like this. Not Jantjie. In his natty suit and tie, Jantjie stood tall and did Jantjie things. The great Obama's sound bites bit the dust. With tripe like:

Hello welcome so far. Well, cigarette join, bringing in different to you. A circle, I would like to pray this offering, basically, this is fun, all of this… balls, to prove this is good, I'm sorry.

Aurally challenged people everywhere were aghast. The game was up. Jantjie was caught and sent packing. An embarrassed government admitted its mistake. The world, fully shocked and entertained, moved on.

Now consider that ace pretender in your office who's been faking it for years. Everyone knows it but the boss. Gift him a framed photo of Thamsanqa Jantjie.

The heroic inspiration and patron saint of every con artist.

*****

A musical morning in Mumbai

In these days of TV talent shows, I doubt if you've gone to a live orchestral music show.

Two years ago, we found ourselves at an official function with live music thrown in.

An aged couple close to us—he was 90, she was 83—were being felicitated by the municipality, along with similar couples, for completing a whopping 60 years of marriage.

We volunteered to take them to the function.

In a touching move to our old couple who were in no position to negotiate the steps leading up to the stage, the officials came down to garland them. They gave mementos and wrapped shawls around them.

And then came the music show.

A dozen musicians arranged themselves in a semi-circle on the stage. Including two harmoniums, one electronic keyboard, a violin, a dholak, a tabla and a guy with two tiny cymbals united by a red thread to do the 'ching-chak.'

There was one elder gentleman who sat among them silently throughout. He must have known the organisers personally to have won the right to be on stage and do nothing.

In the foreground, a singer or two took turns.

It was fabulous. They were a talented, well-knit bunch of senior citizens. They sang unfamiliar (to me) Marathi songs with some popular Hindi ones.

There was no showmanship. The background musicians worked like office clerks poring over their ledgers rather than extroverted Zakir Husains drawing you in with endearing gestures.

Yet the magic of music performed live was unmissable. I don't know what it is about us Indians and music. There are loads of innate musical talent in anonymous places.

The musicians ended strongly with a rousing rendition of Vande Mataram. The audience broke into heavy applause.

And then.

Everyone rushed to the first floor to get free, pre-packed lunch boxes. I don't know what it is about us Indians and food. We go absolutely berserk.

People of all ages pushed and shouted. They thrust their tokens at the attendants from all directions. Everyone jostled to get ahead of everyone else. Mayhem!

The lunch—hard pieces of paneer doused in traffic-light-red curry, an over-spicy vegetable pulao, chapatis made of thin leather and an unknown sweet dish—was not good. But when I looked around, everyone was emptying their boxes rapidly. Food is food.

Frustrated by unruly crowds and bad food, we felt the lovely music of a few moments ago already ebbing away. We drove back in thick Mumbai traffic.

In the front seat, we bickered about the bad behaviour, the lack of civic sense, the noise, how crazy we Indians were…

In the back seat, the old couple were proud of their shawls and mementos. They had enjoyed the music. Even the food was good, they said, although the pulao was a little spicy.

They smiled non-stop and thanked us for the outing itself. "What a lovely morning you gave us," they said.

That brought our smiles back. And suddenly it felt like…

We Indians weren't all that crazy, after all.

* * * * *

Higher studies in London

If you are a student, what gives you away? A table that spills over with books. A table lamp that beams down on a keyboard.

Every book urgent, so all lie cracked open. Neglect everywhere. Empty Maggi packets.

We visited a student couple at the London University in their flat. Would it be different in a foreign land, we wondered.

It was.

Everything was beautifully kept. The sofas were fluffy, free of debris. Books and pens lay on the table and floor, well organised. The bent table lamp was there. And a spotless kitchen to match.

What was the secret of the civilised setup? They had been students before. He was 60 years old. She was 58.

She was doing a management course to advance her skills. He had left his engineering job in the US some years ago and turned a fiction writer. With two published books, he joined an advanced writing course. Touching her greyed temples, she admitted to a mild tension for she had a term paper due the next day.

They offered us a grand choice for lunch: Korean, Japanese, Chinese, Thai, Continental or Indian. While I wondered how they'd rustle up any of those with just some Maggi packs in the kitchen, my wife was quick to grasp the situation.

"Which place is the closest?" she asked.

They treated us to a fabulous lunch at the Thai place. They spoke of their university life. The schedules. The excitement. The daily discoveries.

I was dying to ask the only question that mattered to me: *How did you guys find the motivation to learn formally at such an age?* However, since he was a distant relative I was still getting to know, I didn't force the query.

Some months later, we met again at an old age home in India where his mother was living. I was hoping to get some private time with him to ask my question. His mother was gentle and spoke softly. Her children and grandchildren took turns to visit her from abroad, so she had company all the year round.

I noticed a water colour painting of a wild elephant on her mantelpiece. It was stunning. My friend pointed to his mother.

"She learnt to paint two years ago."

She had quite a collection. She was 85. She had learnt French in her seventies. Now she was planning to publish a book.

My desire to ask my burning question just died. I knew the answer already. It was staring at me. What was your motivation to learn at a later age? Come on. With the towering example that his mother was, did the guy even have a choice?

Her life spoke clearly to all who'd listen. Either you felt you had enough answers. Or you continued to learn new stuff. Life gave you that choice.

It's 2024. She is 86. She published her first book. She came on TV. The subject: Love then and love today.

What she (and her son and wife) will take up next to grapple with in the coming days, I do not know.

*****

Ear piercing in Amsterdam

You make a decision. You execute. And then comes the self-doubt.

In Amsterdam, I went for a stroll with my three young relatives. We crisscrossed quaint bridges over canals. We found ourselves in the famed red-light district. To ease the familial tension in such a context, we joked about this and that.

My niece pointed out how the ladies behind the windows were attractively showcased under a spotlight. We giggled. One woman was engrossed in a book, perhaps a Ludlum bestseller. It all seemed so routine, so normal.

And then, my nephew saw it. A tiny shop with a signboard: Ear Piercing. "How about it," he asked me, excited. Going with the mood of the moment, I said, "Sure." He led the way and we followed him. It was an easy decision.

A thirty-something man, seeing business footfalls walk in, welcomed us with extra wide smiles. He pointed to a stool and put on his green, plastic gloves.

He flicked on a table lamp that cast a powerful beam on me—the kind movie detectives used to extract confessions. He vanished into the darkness and reappeared with a piercing gun. He told me to relax. And there came flooding a rapid series of second thoughts.

Just what the hell was I doing? In this seedy locality full of junkies and pickpockets, why did we pick this hole in the wall? What if the needles were unsterilised? As the older person, shouldn't I be more responsible? You are getting AIDS, I told myself.

The nerviness must have shown. "Look at him having second thoughts. He's worried about the needle prick," my niece laughed. That was true. I was wondering how painful it was going to be.

That guy was good or maybe the gun was hi-tech. I didn't feel a thing, not even a brief sting I was bracing for. Like Jesus before me, I willingly showed him the other cheek, er... ear. He was done in a second. He inserted plastic studs in the ear holes and gave me napkins with antiseptic.

In a minute, my nephew got his piercing done and we walked out into the cool air. We joined the melée of tourists and found a sidewalk cafe to enjoy a cup of coffee.

So, there it was: decision, execution and self-doubt. The threesome I unfailingly encountered in matters big and small.

This one turned out alright. I did not catch any infectious disease. As a bonus, when I returned home, my wife approved the action so much that she got me a tiny diamond stud to replace the plastic one.

This is why, perhaps, I never ever learnt the lesson to not be impulsive.

*****

The way the world works

People have always stolen things. Money, cattle, jewellery. Slaves, idols, art.

In 1928, the painting *Sleeping Lady with a Vase* by a famous Hungarian artist went missing. Decades went by. The artist died in 1953 without a clue.

Years later, in 2009, a guy took his little daughter to watch the Hollywood children's movie *Stuart Little*. He was an art historian. His eyes caught the painting prop on the back wall of a scene.

"I saw Bereny's lost masterpiece behind Hugh Laurie," he said later. "I nearly dropped Lola from my lap."

The film's set designer had seen it in a California antique store and thought it fit for the scene. After the shoot, she sold it to a private art collector and forgot about it.

Thanks to the sharp-eyed movie goer, the story was traced. As a proud artistic nation, Hungary got its treasure back from the collector.

It's satisfying when stolen stuff gets found.

Not just people. Time too steals things from us.

Objects vanish. Rituals vanish. Languages vanish. The script of the ancient Indus Valley Civilisation, for instance, remains a mystery. So do those pretty hieroglyphics of Egypt. Except, they've been decoded recently!

How? How do you retrieve an entire language from Time, the stealer?

In 200 BC, in the time-honoured fashion of Europe ruling over everyone else, the Greeks ruled Egypt. To appease the local people with good public relations, the Greeks got a massive stone tablet made with inscriptions.

In which language should the inscriptions be? The Greek rulers, of course, wrote in Greek. The locals understood a form of early Egyptian called Demotic. And the influential priestly class wrote in formal hieroglyphics.

So, the rulers did what the user manuals of Samsung phones and iPhones do. They wrote in *all* the languages, one underneath the other: hieroglyphics, Demotic and Greek.

Some 2000 years later, in 1799, when Napoleon invaded Egypt—poor Egypt, a new European master to serve now—his troops accidentally found the original tablet in a town called Rosetta. The Rosetta Stone fell into the hands of the Brits when they defeated Napoleon. (Poor Egypt, again.)

No one could understand ancient Demotic or hieroglyphics. But they knew Greek! So, piece by piece, letter by letter, they figured out the script of the two other languages from the one they understood already. It took a few men and some years but the glory of hieroglyphics—it was a proper alphabetic language, not just pictograms as previously thought—was brought to life.

In one case, a guy takes his kid to the movies and ends up retrieving a valuable piece of art.

In another, some soldiers see a huge stone tablet and we end up retrieving an entire, ancient language.

It's good to remind ourselves human progress often comes from random and accidental things.

Never underestimate dumb luck.

*****

Which part of India is your face from?

It used to be easier. No longer. You can't readily tell which part of India someone is from.

See your own reflection in the mirror. The handsome or beautiful face staring back at you can objectively be from one of the many regions in India.

Our regional festivals and special occasions resemble one another more and more with every passing year. Weddings are homogenised. You can't isolate someone if you can't isolate the occasion itself.

I was looking at photos of people on the internet. I also saw their video. Could I place them? Could I, with certainty, say they were from this part of India and not that? No, I couldn't tell.

They wore formal attire. It must have been a festival or family occasion. But location? Was it Pune, Kanpur, Ahmedabad, Mysore or Vijayawada? I couldn't tell.

Consider food. I saw them relishing a formal feast (vegetarian). The presenter showed the menu: things like Alu Gobi, *Chana* (chickpeas), Paneer, Pakora and a cucumber salad.

The fare was North Indian but something about their formal wear suggested the South. (Incidentally, you get good paneer, for instance, in Kanyakumari today. So, you can't identify someone's region from the food alone.)

What if I told you their names? Nandini, Anuradha, Krishnapriya, Madanagopal, Indu, Leela and Kalinda. Didn't help, did it?

Faces. Clothing. Food. Names. I had all the information but was none the wiser. Who were these folks? Where were they from?

When I learnt the answer, I was totally taken aback. Their true origin—get ready—was Sao Paolo.

These folks were Brazilians. They belonged to a Vaishnavite sect and visited India twice a year. They followed all the customs and rituals, including nuanced dress codes and prepared carbon-copy festival dishes.

They didn't speak Hindi or (much) English, only Portuguese. They were vegetarian.

An Indian YouTuber posted a first-hand video of his visit to their temple. It was balanced reportage with no excessive claims about the huge spread of Hinduism worldwide and associated exaggerations. There were a few hundred people in the hall, not millions.

Yet this was remarkable.

Two centuries ago, Samuel Johnson noted—if you disregard the inherent sexism of those times— "a woman's preaching is like a dog's walking on his hind legs. It is not done well; but you are surprised to find it done at all."

In the case of Indian rituals being carried out by locals in faraway Brazil, it was certainly surprising to find it done at all. Unlike Johnson's case, it was done well too. The details were xerox-worthy.

I didn't have more than passing interest in the subject to dig deeper. Of how it all started, where and when. (Google 'Sao Paolo Hindus' if you want to follow through.)

But I was gobsmacked all the same.

How could religious rituals travel to a continent like South America with whom we shared no historical bond, no common language and no migrations of substance?

Only God knew.

*****

When old people travel

Things happen at an airport while we wait.

A smart, young lady announced the boarding at our gate. Elderly people—some in their 80s—were told to form a queue. Two were in wheelchairs with attendants. Others stood up and shuffled across to make a line.

For 20 minutes in the middle of the hall, in silence, they waited for further instructions. It wasn't clear why they were standing when they could have been sitting.

No one complained. A few of us, watching this and feeling antsy, stood up to complain. But mercifully, the queue started moving. We fell silent. There was a further wait of 10 minutes for the elderly inside the aerobridge as the flight was "being readied to receive" the passengers.

Once on the plane, a tired old lady found it difficult to lift and place her cabin baggage. The hostess pointed to empty spaces but did not offer physical help.

My wife lifted her bag and put it in the bin. I mumbled something about being a little too far away to assist (my 'convenient distancing' came up for scrutiny and discussion a while later, but I digress.)

The hostess said she wasn't allowed by airline rules to touch a passenger's luggage. If true, it was a sad reflection on an airline that prided itself on passenger comfort.

It also struck me that the airport crew at the counter were so young. Six of them, all in their twenties. One of them threw his hands about, raised his voice and generally played the leader's role. Young, cocky and managerial.

When you are 25, you are not thinking about a day when you will be 70. That day is too far off.

You hardly worry about old folks standing still in one place for 20 minutes as being any kind of inconvenience.

On the other hand, when you're past 70, you understand stuff. You've been there before.

Which probably explains why none of the elderly people seemed particularly perturbed. Bent and stooping, they stared at some indeterminate point on the floor ahead of them, conserving energy, unmoving.

To people in the hall who were mostly between the two age extremes, it was uncomfortable to watch—the forbearance of the elderly in tandem with the hustle and swagger of youth, while dealing with their own emotions, watching. Should they act on the anger rising inside? Or stay silent because this too shall pass?

A senior airline executive somewhere could have put a simple process in place and taken care of everything. Don't make old people stand up unless you intend to keep them moving.

How much rocket science can this be?

*****

Commercial Street, Bengaluru

Before there were malls, there were whole streets that did the job. In Bengaluru, for instance, you had Commercial Street.

It had everything—hairbrushes, coffee powder, Arrow shirts, Bengali sweets, school uniforms, steel utensils, veggies, steam irons, Amrutanjan and Crocin, beanbag refills, jocks and socks, cooker gaskets, Kerala *papads*, sticker bindis, shoe laces, et al.

You knew where to get a rubber stamp. And where to get your grandfather's photograph framed. My own forte was where to get superb ice cream.

No escalators. No air-conditioning. Not many fancy shops. Dust and noise. For added interest, cycles, carts and cows came at you. You walked a lot because of the random distances between the shops you visited on a given evening. Prices were whatever you and the shopkeepers agreed on.

My job, then as now, was to carry stuff. I was also the designated rider. Walking back from serious shopping, I once saw a balloon seller at the corner with a striking collection. My wife nudged me to stop staring and go get the bike from the parking place.

When I came back on my Yezdi bike to pick her up, the balloon guy had advanced to the next level—of making crazy animal shapes. Poodles, rabbits, cats and such. I wanted a balloon animal for myself. But we did not have a child then for an excuse. We quietly rode away without buying any.

Talking on a bike with a helmet on is never easy. You're not sure if you're being heard, so you shout. I yelled at my wife that I loved those balloons. The skill, the bright colours and the rapid execution. Great stuff, I told her.

Like with the mobile phone these days—you are talking away, and suddenly it feels like there is no one at the other end—as if the line got disconnected a while ago. On my bike ride home that evening, shouting into the wind, I got an eerie feeling I was alone.

I waved a free arm behind me and felt no resistance. Just the cool, Bengaluru air. She couldn't have fallen off (people in the dense traffic would have alerted me.) It was obvious. I had failed to pick her up and *vrooomed* off alone.

I returned to the corner. The balloon seller had vanished. My wife stood with the bags. I stopped sheepishly and mumbled something about being fairly certain she had climbed on. How come she delayed getting on?

"Sure," she said, "it must be my fault." The tone was sharp.

But, wait, what was the pink thing poking out of a shopping bag? "It's a balloon poodle," she said. "Cheesy as hell. But I thought you'd like it."

That's the way it turns out sometimes. You forget someone in haste and they repay you with a gift.

Like I was saying, shopping streets are different. Malls are different. I hardly have any mall memories. But shopping street memories?

I have tons.

* * * * *

4

Work

Decaf

SELF-HELP GURUS TELL you to take confident decisions even when you don't have all the information.

Act with what you have. Don't wait for perfect information which may never come. Be bold.

Many years ago, a bigwig from the head office visited one of the minor colonies—our Bengaluru office.

Ajit had returned from a training stint abroad. He also returned with an accent and an affected mannerism or two. All of us gathered in the conference room to listen to Ajit's state of the nation address.

Sundar, the pantry guy, came in to take orders.

Sundar was an expert in South Indian decoction coffee. Everyone asked for coffee except for a couple of die-hard tea loving Malayalis.

Ajit signalled to Sundar. "Decaf," he said.

Decaffeinated coffee was a big thing abroad then. It was available in a few pockets locally—grey-market shops in posh areas at fat prices.

But it was a novel request. Many of us didn't even know what he was talking about. We looked at Sundar with curiosity.

Sundar calmly repeated everyone's orders. And turned to Ajit to confirm his.

"I told you. Bring me decaf," said Ajit, curtly. As the guy left the room, Ajit called him back. "You got it, pal? Decaf. Not the regular shit."

Sundar nodded and fled.

Ajit made a presentation on our ad agency's future. He showed graphs and numbers. He called out Bengaluru's non-performance. His Indian accent photo bombed his US accent. He kept saying 'karode' for 'crore.'

It was a curse that a single misshapen word often blew up our subterfuge and exposed our true identity beneath. Sundar came with a massive tray and a fabulous aroma of freshly made coffee. Proceedings stopped. We shuffled water glasses and notepads to make room for the cups.

Ajit let his coffee cool. Or forgot about it. When he finally took a sip, it was a hefty one. His cheeks bulged.

His face froze in shock.

He rushed out with pouted lips and puffed cheeks. Our manager followed him to the loo. Low as I was on the food chain, I too ran along in the guise of helping.

He spat it out. He coughed. He spat more. He cursed. He coughed more.

It turned out that Sundar, the king of coffee, had interpreted the meaning of decaf his own way.

Decaf. Tea-caff. Tea-coffee. Aha! Let's combine both.

Sundar took his famous coffee decoction and added a normal cup of tea to it. He knew better than to argue in life. If some big shot wanted unusual stuff, who was he to question it?

Ajit said it was the worst coffee he had ever had in his life.

We advised Sundar to avoid the conference room for the immediate future.

He had taken a bold, innovative decision based on limited information given in a mock US accent. And somehow, inadvertently, created a memorable piece of office lore for all times to come.

Perhaps, the self-help gurus are right, after all.

NOTE: This is based on what a colleague told me years ago. And the 'I' here is the colleague. A few have chimed in since to say this really happened. It makes for a good story, in any case.

*****

Everyday superstitions

In my corporate life, I wore a lucky shirt to an important presentation. For extra luck, I had a shave with the spare razor stashed in my desk drawer.

A client reopened a finished website project to overturn the entire colour scheme: please make it all *sindoor*-red and turmeric yellow as advised by our family guru.

A colleague ejected himself out of the lift in the nick of time to return to his cabin and touch a piece of zari from his late grandmother before hurrying on to his client meeting.

This sort of thing can get powerful and big. Imagine this.

An African tribesman—or Javanese hunter or Native American or a tribal in Central India, choose your pick—from a thousand years ago, steps out of his hut in the morning, inserts a lazy finger in his nostril and looks up to the sky. Black clouds gather and rain falls copiously on the parched land.

The news spreads. The village is joyous. And the belief grows that for rains to fall in abundance, the trick is to insert a finger in the right nostril in the morning while stepping out of your hut. They make it into a ritual dance. And the nostril dance lingers for centuries.

We are ingenious as a human race. We are very good at creating stories and beliefs. Even a rational mind like the scientist Arthur Eddington had a horseshoe in his study for good luck. (*I'm told it works whether you believe in it or not.*)

The great Sachin insisted that teammates did not leave their chairs during tense moments in a match to prevent losing.

International cricketers have been known to wear their left padding first (or similar) to score big. Whether tribesmen, scientists, sportsmen or mid-level managers, we need results. But we don't know the future. There is no guarantee.

Rains may not fall, experiments may end in failure, we may get out the first ball in cricket, or the client may reject our work. But then, as we all know, we sometimes succeed. Rains pour, a breakthrough is made, a century is scored, and the client loves our idea. Magic!

That's when we say to ourselves, I knew it! This thing really works. My ancestral zari cloth, my left padding, my ritual dance, my lucky shirt is the reason for my success!

Just for that—just for the hope it offers us in managing an unknowable future, a superstition or two feels so comforting. Rationally unnecessary, emotionally steadying.

The ultimate emotional argument: Where's the harm? Who am I hurting? The ultimate defensive argument: What's *your* problem, man? It works for me.

So, knock yourself out. Buy the car with a registration that adds up to 9. Make your sofas, shoes and stationery the same shade of pink. Add an extra 'R' to your name. Wear your lucky shirt to a meeting. Begin a flight of stairs with your left foot.

Whatever floats your boat.

* * * * *

Selling lottery tickets

A long career in advertising exposes you to many product categories. Except for lottery tickets, in my case.

In the nineties, every state had its own lottery scheme. Habitual buyers needed no persuasion and those opposed to lottery in principle were immune to persuasion.

As always, the real opportunity lay with the majority in the middle. No strong opinions either way. They could be persuaded.

One of the best campaigns came from the New York office of the multinational agency I worked for. Every TV ad for New York Lotto showed a regular person living it up with the money they'd won.

In one ad, for instance, an elderly lady, knitting quietly at home, hired the entire New York Philharmonic orchestra to play for an audience of one—herself.

In another ad, a young man's rude ex-boss suggested, "You are probably pumping gas somewhere now, no doubt." To which the guy coolly replied, "How did you know? I just bought an oil company."

The ads ended with a killer tag line: *Hey, you never know.*

As one of the popular taglines in US advertising, it triggered the classic what-if daydream in thousands of folks who made up the middle. With the right mixture of humour and believability, the ads disarmed the fence straddlers.

In the movie *Dumb & Dumber*, Jim Carey's penniless character asked his love interest, an heiress: "What are the odds of someone like me ending up with someone like you?" She replied, "About one in a million." And he went, "So you're saying there's a chance!"

Hey, you never know. (Until you try.)

In the Mumbai of the 90's, the Maharashtra government had their lottery scheme with a strong tag line. In jingle form the priceless words were: *Aaj nahi toh kal.* If not today, tomorrow.

Good lines have a way of cutting through the crap and getting to the heart of things in double-quick time. In any language. In four words, the anonymous writer brought alive the potential benefit of repeat purchases!

The nearest I came to buying a lottery ticket myself was when I was stuck at the traffic lights in a cab.

A street vendor held a fanned-out spread of lottery tickets. One ticket, with the promise of a few crores, left his grasp, wafted in the wind and landed in my lap. Surely, it was a sign from above. But, untrusting, I returned it to the man.

The next moment, I changed my mind.

I popped my head out of the window to call him back. And I saw him, with practised ease, let go of a ticket 'accidentally' into the wind. It wafted into the window of the car behind. Smart move!

My cab driver smiled at me in the rearview mirror. And we went on our way.

Damn. Lottery tickets can be so very irresistible if a customer buys the idea rather than being sold to.

Like everything else.

* * * * *

A culture of bribes

Bribes, anyone? In the advertising industry, some creative directors were known to give commercial projects to film directors who gave them a cut.

I knew reputed creative directors who did this. Their reasoning: I'm choosing you over other good choices. We both are adults here. Let me partake of your good fortune.

Years ago, a copywriter's pipe-dream of an 'Open on a beach in France…' type script got approved for me. The director suggested Cape Town. It was cheaper. The client agreed.

His team worked the details and sent me my visa-stamped passport. The envelope also contained $500 in crisp notes, a huge amount for its time.

At the first pre-shoot meeting, I returned the money. He was surprised. "Why? Just buy something for your son, man."

I said that my company paid me well enough to buy toys, not to worry.

"Cool," he shrugged. We moved on. We had a great shoot. I also worked with him on a couple of projects in later years. All smooth. No suggestion of kickbacks.

On the other hand, there was this top-notch director who was clean as a whistle, no dodgy stuff and brilliant at work. I loved working with him time and again.

After eight or nine successful projects in a row, I was happy with the high quality work and stellar results. However, I wasn't aware that my repeated collaborations with the same director was making the higher-ups in my company suspicious of my motives.

My manager, wondering if I was on the take, sent his secretary to meet with me.

She said, "Boss was asking if we're going with the same company for this project also?"

Seeing red, I broke into the manager's cabin. "It's not what you think," I told him bluntly. "I'm not taking any money from XYZ to do our films with them. That guy is fantastic, that's all."

It was a dumb thing to do. No one had accused me of anything. And there I was, defending already. Just the kind of thing a guilty person might do.

He calmly pushed his chair on coasters away from me. "Sure, Narayan," he said, placing all pointy fingers under his chin. His faint smile said: Do you take me for an idiot?

I left his room, defeated. I never sorted it out with him in later years. You cannot solve what isn't raised.

Years later, I jumped a red light in Mumbai and a traffic cop moved with alacrity from the side of the road. I braked. As he approached, my son, all of 10 years old, piped up. "He wants a bribe."

I slid the glass down. The cop gave me an oily smile and said, "Licence?" as a conversation starter.

I reached for my back pocket and realised—yet again!—I'd forgotten my wallet at home. I gave the cop my own oily, sheepish smile. He was aghast.

"You're going to his school and your office but you don't have your purse?" he said, looking dejected. I nodded. He straightened up and waved me off. My forgetfulness saved me 50 bucks. In the rear mirror, I saw him wryly laughing at his bad luck.

Bribes everywhere. Some take, others don't. Some accuse, everyone gives.

Just another day in colourful, let's-get-it-done India.

*****

The art of grabbing attention

You expect advertising to go out and grab its audience. In other creative pursuits too, the story is the same.

If you dance, sing or paint very well, you expect your art will grab enough people. But it doesn't work like that. It is your consumer, not you, who decides whether to grab your stuff or not.

A whole generation grabbed onto Tendulkar's artistry. As they did the art of Ravi Shankar and Satyajit Ray.

For millions of us non-Picassos, non-Federers and non-Subbulakshmis, the rules are the same. We may be skilled in our own way but our audience gets to deliver the verdict. Not us.

Last week, there was a *kavi sammelan* in our housing society organised by the Senior Citizens Group. The poets were senior citizens and so was the audience.

We accompanied an elderly woman in her 80's to the function. She was looking forward to an evening of poetry, snacks and friends. What fun!

A crowd of a few hundred sat on hired plastic chairs on the podium. The hubbub was loud, the atmosphere expectant. No better time for a local poet to come on stage and shine.

There were quite a few of them. Including someone who read out her Tamil poem and did a Hindi translation as well. She fished out another piece of paper and read the English translation too, just in case.

The well-known local poets pulled rank and placed themselves later down the order. Newer poets were thrust out ahead.

Everyone cheered. Who doesn't love poetry? Even if no Tagores or Mirabais were on display, who cared? The enthusiasm was high.

At some point, the heady aroma of fresh *bhajias* wafted by. The good stuff came in a mix of onion, potato, cauliflower and palak variants. Bearers from a nearby restaurant marched to a make-shift food counter to place their precious cargo. All watched their movements with interest.

The bearers took a good look at the average age of the assemblage. To avoid a stampede among aged folk, they reached each one personally.

Suddenly, paper plates were everywhere. Each *bhajia* variant had its own adherents.

On stage, the more accomplished poets realised they were losing the audience by the second. The traitorous audience had traded their deep art for deep-fried snacks. No one was listening.

Various elderly cries of "Cauliflower here!" and "Onion over here!" rent the air. Some poets gamely slowed their pace and repeated their lines to gain attention. But the *bhajias* won. What, after all, was art in front of food?

While dropping our elderly member after the festivities, we asked her how it went. She beamed fully after 85 sprightly years on the planet. "The *bhajias* were tasty!" she summarised.

After a minute of deep reflection, she confessed impishly. "I took a whole handful of the onion ones."

Like I said, consumers decide what to grab.

* * * * *

Bees on the Expressway

Everyone doesn't see what you see. Even when it's obvious to you. Years ago, a colleague and I were on the relatively new Mumbai-Pune Expressway for a client meeting.

It was a lovely, smooth drive we looked forward to.

I said, "Wonder when they are going to remove all these beehives."

"What beehives?" He was curious.

"Those huge beehives at the entrance of tunnels."

"What beehives at tunnel entrances?" He was surprised.

He kept his eyes peeled for the next tunnel.

"Oh, look at those beehives!" he said. "There's a huge bunch of them."

He became hooked. He observed every tunnel after that and turned back to check the other side too after passing through. "So many beehives! How come in all our trips you never mentioned this?"

"I thought everyone knew."

He asked the driver. The driver hadn't seen them before.

Next day, back at the office, my colleague conducted an informal poll. "Had any of you people noticed beehives on the Mumbai-Pune Expressway?"

And the unanimous response was: No.

He was relieved. He was happy to find out he was normal. He later told me that he had pointed out the beehives to everyone he travelled with to Pune. None had seen them before.

It puzzled me no end that what I'd noticed for years was part of no one else's observation. Was I a bee keeper in my previous birth?

It took a while to figure out the answer. It was one word.

PowerPoint.

Everyone—at least those in my industry—was invariably busy using the travel time to juggle their presentation slides for the meeting. Their adrenalin and single-minded focus would kick in as they usually do when one works at the last minute.

There could be bees flying about outside the size of piglets for all they cared. They were zoning out in their work. They constantly said things like, "Check this out, I'm doing the first part differently" and "Do you want a slide that says Creative before you come in?"

I know it's a small thing. Noticing beehives is not a big deal. They are not like spotting lions in the Savannah. There's no *paisa vasool.* No employer will be impressed and give you an increment for observing them.

Yet.

It's nice to use travel time for travel. And let the world come to you.

Looking at the hard-working, committed and ambitious people out there, I sometimes wonder if we have lost a lovely art form along the way.

The art of idling.

P.S: Some time after the pandemic, the beehives were removed from all the tunnels. My well networked colleague might have spread the word far enough to reach the authorities.

*****

Locked out of a German car

When you buy something expensive like a high-end car, you expect excellent service. It's only fair.

Some years ago, I convinced myself I should indulge in a fancy, German car.

Till one day it didn't work. The doors wouldn't unlock. I couldn't get inside the car. It was 8 pm and the car was parked on a side road near the office.

Our office assistant, who carried my bags, watched silently as I pressed the remote key. Nothing unlocked. (I hate it when other people carry my bags. But this dude was always adamant.)

I called the service person. He advised that I use the manual key hidden inside the remote key. How clever, I thought. I fished it out but it didn't work. I told the guy the manual key was jamming. He asked me if I had turned the key clockwise or anti-clockwise.

"Both," I replied.

"Not possible," he said.

Icily, I told him he should call a senior engineer to help me. I was getting the worst service possible for an expensive product. I gave him half an hour to come up with a solution.

I headed back to office and piled onto Chinese food that late-working colleagues had ordered for themselves.

The service person called and begged me to go to the car right away.

"Insert the manual key," he said, "and turn it anti-clockwise very s-l-o-w-l-y."

My office assistant aimed his phone torch at the keyhole. I turned the key very s-l-o-w-l-y. Nothing happened. It jammed as before. I lost it. I raved at the service chap. I promised I would speak to his manager the next morning.

I decided to call a cab.

Just then, a vague mental picture took shape in my mind and gathered focus.

When I parked my car that morning, I noticed the front wheels were over a speed breaker hump and the back wheels were behind the hump. I even enjoyed the cheap thrill of parking my car in that manner.

Now, looking down, I saw there was no speed breaker under the car. I rushed to the front of the car to check the registration. The numbers were all wrong.

This was not my car! Same German brand, same flashy red—but not mine.

Down the road, about a dozen cars away, I spotted mine lit by a street lamp. Signalling my assistant to come along, I kept it all cool and walked extra casually.

Driving home, I got a concerned call from the service guy. "Chill," I said to him. All under control now. I discouraged further probing.

Next morning, the receptionist smiled. "We heard," she said. Colleagues popped their heads out of cabins like meerkats and laughed like jackasses.

It was that silent assistant—or was he the silent assassin?—who spread the word across the entire office. About what was frankly a private matter between me and my car.

Moral: Never let an assistant carry your bags.

P.S: To my credit, I apologised to the service guy later. He now runs his own ice cream parlour in Bengaluru. Bless him.

*****

Creating brand names

The fun of advertising is that sometimes you get an opportunity to have your personal say in professional matters. Sometimes.

Long ago, a big industrial group wanted a brand name for their forthcoming range of premium suitings.

As a cub writer, it was a time when I knew no one in Mumbai. With no friends, I sunk all my non-working hours into learning the classical guitar. Reading musical notation and translating squiggles on the score to frets on the instrument was slow going.

The next morning, I wrote "C-Major" in my company-issued notepad with my company-issued ball pen.

The Copy Chief read it and took me to meet the MD. "Tell him." So, I told him the name I had scribbled.

The MD, who didn't even know who I was, picked up the intercom and called in some people: the Account Director, the Media Director and a few other bigwigs. "Tell them," the MD instructed. I told them.

After a moment of silent cud-chewing, the room broke into smiles. Short of dancing on tables, everyone said the client would love it. So different, so premium. What a name.

This advertising business, I concluded, was too easy. I could do this blind-folded.

A week later, consumer research bombed the idea. The Research Director told us he personally thought the name was great, nodding warmly in my direction. But the consumers didn't care for it. When asked to free-associate with the name C-Major, the consumer groups basically said, "Music."

Which, if you thought about it, was pretty obvious and predictable. Anyone familiar with Western music would associate C-Major with music.

It was like asking people to free-associate with the word Hollywood. They would certainly say "Movies," not "Suitings." Why? Because there weren't any brand of suitings called *Hollywood.* Yet.

The Research Director, shaking his head sadly in my direction, summed it up: no one free-associated the word C-Major with suitings. Instead, everyone associated it with music. Therefore, we should drop C-Major as a brand name for suitings because it did not remind anyone of suitings!

I could not believe my ears. It was like naming something "Cadbury" for the first time and expecting consumers en masse to associate it with "Yes! Chocolates!" I mean, why would they? It took time to build a brand and proper associations.

These advertising grown-ups, I concluded, were full of shit.

Years later, in a different agency in a different city, a chain of computer stores was moving into software big time. The Account Director told me they wanted a name for the new company. "Something different," he said. "Nothing with 'data', 'tech' or 'info' in it."

My musical struggles had yielded fruit over time. I was in Grade 6, which wasn't too bad. That morning, my chosen torture was working out a tough piece called Sonata in B Minor.

It came easily off the pen. I scribbled "Sonata" in the notepad. It certainly sounded different for a software company. My art guy placed a neat little graphic of a piano keyboard under the serif in all capitals. Both the name and logo went through like a shot in a single meeting between our AD and their head honcho.

Mercifully, no one researched the name for free associations. It took its time but the scorecard eventually showed a draw.

Fate - 1, Narayan - 1.

* * * * *

Buying a phone online

I eagerly awaited the annual Diwali festive season sale from Amazon. My phone's audio was crackling and I was forced to use the speaker for every call. Irritating. I needed a new one.

The day of the launch, I logged in. I was asked about my brand, the model and its IMEI number (they gave me instructions how to find it.)

I got a ₹2,100 exchange price. I loved price offs. They would deliver it the next day.

Next morning, Amazon mailed me. Back up your phone data and clear your personal stuff off it before you hand it over. Sure. I did as told.

I then noticed they had shifted the delivery date to later in the week. I had already cleared the contacts list! For the next 4 days, I found myself receiving calls from 10-digit numbers instead of friends, associates and spammers. I ended up intercepting known folks with, "Who is this?"

The day came. The phone rang but stopped before I could answer it. I called back. An automated lady from a central Amazon facility informed me that their attempted delivery could not be completed. She said I could speak to the delivery agent—after entering the 4-digit PIN. What 4-digit PIN?

In the mails and messages, I found a 6-digit password to give the delivery guy but no 4-digit PIN. After re-reading some more, I found it buried in the text.

The delivery guy came on the line. I asked him why he didn't deliver. My call was not answered, he said. I will come tomorrow.

Next day. A delivery guy turned up to say he had to wait for a 'technical' guy to approve the package. He joined us 45 minutes later.

He asked me for the 4-digit PIN. I readily gave him. But it didn't work. He wanted a different one. I didn't have a different one. He gave me his own phone that showed some instructions. I had to re-install the Amazon app on my phone, login and feed in a 6-digit code from his phone. In return, Amazon kindly gave me a 4-digit PIN which I offered him.

He scrutinised my phone. He pointed to a faint hairline on the bottom right of the screen. It's cracked, he said. I told him that it wasn't even visible. But he insisted I pay the full price.

The delivery guy watched us keenly, nodding in agreement with whoever was talking. It must have been a welcome diversion from a dull day at work. I was exhausted. I told them to get lost.

I turned up at the Samsung store nearby and got a ₹3,500 exchange price. The nice guy there transferred my SIM, my data and offered coffee. He noticed the same hairline on the screen but agreed it was not visible.

It was all good in the end. So, was there a sense of victory or relief? Elation that I got a bigger discount? Not really. For I had already paid my dues in time, effort and exhaustion.

Nothing comes for free.

*****

Nearby questions

It's puzzling. The way we answer questions at work or play. We don't answer the question we are asked. Instead, we answer a nearby question.

Someone shares their vacation plans. "Anything interesting to do in Portugal?" And we answer, "Hungary is great fun! Budapest is awesome."

The question is about Portugal. But we change it to a nearby question on Hungary. Why? Because we know how to answer it.

Forgetting momentarily the word 'croutons', I ask my colleague. "What's the name of those bread things you put in soups?" He says, "Don't have soups any more. Prefer salads."

Thank you. But my question was not, "What are your food habits?"

A little girl asks, "Does the equator pass through Tanzania?" I lecture her about the magical, annual wildebeest migration.

I was answering the nearby question of "What makes Tanzania special?" Which is not what she asked, but what I knew. (As a bonus, I tell her that a wildebeest is also called a gnu.)

Sometimes, we don't want trouble.

"You told Ajay we're not coming?" asks the wife. The guy answers, "Their little Anshu is not well."

Which is an answer to a question not asked at all.

"Asthma again?" says the concerned wife. They discuss the health of their friends' child. The husband, like thousands before him, thereby successfully evades the original question. For which the troublesome answer is: No, I forgot to call Ajay.

It happens at work too. (You can tell I'm a fan of Kahneman's *Thinking, Fast and Slow*.)

Did the client approve the strategy? And someone replies, "I hear his junior is being promoted over him." Everyone leans in to get the latest gossip. Strategy approval? Never mind, *yaar*.

I point to a random dog and ask my friend, "Is that a terrier or a bulldog?" He takes a look and says, "Pomeranians are the worst. My neighbour has one." He mimics its crazy, high-pitched barking multiple times. We laugh. The random dog's breed remains unknown.

A group of friends discuss cricket. Someone asks, "Anyone knows who Hardik Pandya's coach is?" Another replies, "We lived 3 buildings away from Ramakant Achrekar (Tendulkar's coach.)" Really? What was he like? Was he humble? Tell us more. Forget Hardik.

Ask someone today: "Got your iPhone 16 Pro?"

A true Nearby Question Expert will confidently say, "Man, what a mile-long queue at the Apple Store! Kids today have so much money or what?" The conversation opens out, everyone chips in and the Expert escapes from giving a straight answer.

Hearing real questions but answering nearby questions instead is a quick, instinctive art.

To get out of awkward situations ("So how old is the birthday girl today?") or hide our inaction ("Did you send the proposal?") or avoid our status being judged ("Which car do you drive?").

Often, though, I think it is a refusal to admit ignorance—whether about dogs or croutons or Tanzania—and simply saying:

I don't know.

*****

Office attire

When someone does something different from the usual in office, it raises eyebrows. It gets people's tongues wagging. It makes them wonder why.

Long back, there was this head of department in my agency with a noticeable trait.

He never tucked in his shirt; it was always out.

Unlike us, boys and girls, in the creative department who wore just about anything anyhow, the business types were usually well turned out. Many wore ties.

But this gentleman, let's call him TD, for all his seniority and formal airs, never wore a tie nor tucked his shirt in.

Then, suddenly, on a certain Wednesday…

TD turned up for work with his shirt tucked in!

It caused a flutter among the secretaries who spread the word to everyone. Even someone as self-absorbed and aloof as me went for a stroll to sneak a look at TD in his cabin.

It was true. He was looking all smart and tucked in.

Possible theories began to float. Had TD found a significant other in his life for all his conservative demeanour? Perhaps TD did it for the big pitch (multinational client) coming up in the afternoon.

Or the higher ups in our food chain finally decided to chastise TD for his sartorial waywardness and insisted on a 'proper' dress code. Maybe he had decided to give up his boring look once and for all and turned a new leaf.

No one dared ask him directly for he was way too senior and too severe a personality. Till our Branch Manager dropped by after lunch and took one look at him.

"Oi, TD," he exclaimed. "What's with the new tucked in look?"

And TD, much to our collective curiosity, answered the Question of the Day quite easily.

"Nothing, man," he said. "Today, instead of wearing my trousers first, I wore my shirt first!"

That was it. So much for all our complicated theories.

As often happened, there was always a hidden and simpler explanation for everything.

Something too simple to deduce.

* * * * *

Environmentally friendly

Ask any experienced marketer or communications pro. They will tell you to be clear rather than clever. Say it exactly the way you want it to be understood.

It's not easy to achieve. In a large, multi-lingual country like India, ambiguity resides around every corner.

Years ago, a well-respected company launched a detergent powder that in concept and formulation was way ahead of its time. It contained no chemicals that were harmful to the environment. This was a brave company coming out with a socially conscious, everyday product. Quite heroic, really. It was a pity though that there was no general awareness among consumers about environmental issues then, not at least at the popular level.

Subjects like global warming, climate crisis and river pollution entered popular consciousness many years later.

As their agency, we were tasked with launching it, highlighting 'environmentally friendly' as its promise to a world that didn't care about any such thing. One of the key decisions taken was to place 'Phosphate-free' upfront on the pack below the brand name in a prominent font size. It would make the intent clear. While TV and print did the heavy lifting of conveying the key benefit, the pack itself would serve as a reminder of a responsible brand choice.

It was a tough campaign to do convincingly. But the product was getting picked up in key markets in good numbers. That was a relief. Probably, the environmental messaging did work, after all. Or, more likely, it was the well-respected corporate name behind the product that carried the day.

However, the thing I remember the most about this campaign was an oddball research report that came in. Oddball reports are always interesting. Apparently, some customers in a city in Bihar bought the detergent, scanned the pack graphics and demanded free phosphate! They pointed to the 'Phosphate Free' blurb and asked for their share. The report did not say anything about how shopkeepers handled these requests.

Rest assured that your best efforts at clarity will be misunderstood by someone somewhere. It's guaranteed. You can't win them all. Accept it. It's a cross every communicator must bear.

There was a silver lining, though. As a young professional, I learnt indelibly that the word 'Free' was magic. Whether in North or South India 'Free' always worked.

It sold product. Why else would random folks in Bihar demand phosphate? Why would you even ask for the damn thing when you had no idea what you'd do with it?

You really want to know? Because it's free, boss.

That's why.

*****

Clients will be clients

We feel a certain way. Our clients feel it another way. Tension. Conflict.

Everyone knows the drill. Stay logical, breathe deeply, be diplomatic. All of which is tough to do in the real world.

I wasn't good at handling creative differences. Till I learnt it from a couple of masters along the way.

Years ago, a client decided to share his strong opinion in the middle of an expensive TV commercial shoot. He had been sitting quietly for hours as the scene was being set up. He even cracked jokes.

After a surfeit of dried fruit and sundry juices (they feed you well on shoots), his mood changed. He perhaps felt himself becoming soft and weak, and the urge to reassert his aggressive self must have surfaced.

It was an elaborate setup involving fifty junior artistes (you don't say 'extras' any more) on platforms at various heights.

The brand was a world-famous sports shoe/apparel brand. The foreground was meant to feature two star cricketers doing their thing, who were currently relaxing in the vanity van outside.

It took 3 hours to set up. As the cameras were about to roll, the client piped up. He asked me if the whole front row of artistes at the ground level could be dispensed with.

It didn't make sense. It would leave a big gap and upset the balance of everything so carefully set up.

Perhaps he was feeling the disruptive energy of the steady stream of coconut pieces and almonds he'd been hogging.

I was about to spout a brief lecture to dissuade him. That's just the kind of thing real Masters do *not* do.

The director of the film—an award-winning, experienced, respected Master—sitting ahead of us turned around. He had heard the client.

"You think the front line should disappear?"

"It's distracting," said the client. "Do we need it really?" He spoke politely but firmly.

What did the Master do? He walked up to the main stage and cleared out the front row. His team shifted the props to take care of the gap nicely.

In 15 minutes, he rejoined us. All three of us stared intently at the new setup on the TV monitor. That's when the Master gestured and spoke softly.

He gently shook his head, unconvinced. "Not working, no? You guys think this works?" he softly enquired.

The client spoke. "Nah, it doesn't work. I prefer the original setup actually."

The front row came back. Problem solved. The Master knew the secret. Never put down a client's opinion, especially in a group.

That was not all. Go a step further. Take the suggestion seriously and execute it. State your opinion *after* having done the work.

Don't lecture. Don't object. Just do and show. The rest of the shoot went like a dream.

I made my mental notes. And realised clearly why Masters were Masters.

For my part, I showed my client more glass jars on the table behind the ones he was raiding. They contained cashews, walnuts, Shrewsbury biscuits, banana chips and dates.

To help him chill in the full knowledge that he was in capable hands.

* * * * *

Jain & Iyer

Some brand names start life with a clear definition. Names like International Business Machines, Fair & Lovely and Life Insurance of India. But most don't have any meaning.

Names like Mahindra, Amul and Cadbury's didn't automatically mean vehicles, butter and chocolates when they started. And a name like Google didn't mean anything at all, least of all a search engine.

Yesterday, a local brand—extremely local, available only in a couple of suburbs of Mumbai—sent across our weekly supplies of ready-to-pour idli batter. We'd been buying that brand for 15 years, probably more. It was called Jain & Iyer.

In that time, we'd seen the range expand to dosa batter, vada batter, coconut chutney, gunpowder, sambar and rasam powder, wheat flour, rava idli mix, upma mix, dhoklas, khakhras, nachni chips, quinoa puffs, jowari chivda, cookies, etc.

My own favourites: Jain & Iyer Idli Batter. And Jain & Iyer Jowari Chivda. World class! It was an intriguing brand name too.

The story went like this: Two friends in college, one from Rajasthan and the other from Palghat, watched movies together, shared jokes, hung out a lot. The Iyer guy loved making idlis. And Jain, true to his stereotype, had business in his blood.

After college, it was only natural they pooled their talent. They targeted the central suburbs of Matunga and Wadala. Their product: idli batter, of course. The localities had a huge number of South Indians and Gujaratis (who as a rule enjoy South Indian food big time.)

It made sense. Iyer made the stuff. Jain sold the stuff. Each worked his competence.

A cool tale of strange bedfellows with no common language or backgrounds making it big together. An atypical case so typical of Mumbai. Maximum city. You felt nice eating their stuff.

And that was the story.

It's a story I made up. In bits and pieces over time. I had not met them or read about them, didn't know who they were and wouldn't recognise them if we shared an elevator. I didn't know if either or both were male or female.

But I liked my story. I didn't take the trouble of getting their real story by meeting them. I didn't want to know. Why?

I dreaded finding out Jain was actually the gourmet cook and Iyer the shrewd business wizard. That would destroy my symmetry. What if both were management graduates who hired professional cooks? That ruined the bromance.

Or, they really were Punjabis who thought up a canny name to appeal to the communities they lived among. Terrible.

Stories were nice. Truths were boring or worse. Facts mustn't get in the way of a satisfying fiction.

For this reason, I will never visit a Paper Boat facility or an Apple production line in Thailand or wherever. I don't want to see anything that messes up my idea of what those brands mean to me.

So, what's in a brand name, you say? Everything you want it to be.

NOTE: *It turned out that the story I made up was, in a general sense, more or less true. Except that the two partners were women, not men.*

*****

5

Things

Before there were mobile phones

YOU MAY OR may not know this depending on your age. Before there were mobile phones, there were pagers. Little black boxes that beeped you messages.

Bosses and folks in sales wore a pager on their belts. When it beeped in company, they stared at the message in an important way. As if to say, "I don't know about you. But I happen to be a busy person." And they looked for the nearest phone.

That was the other thing. Before there were mobile phones, there were telephones. The moneyed had answering machines. If you're older than a dinosaur, you will recall the black, rotary dials in offices and privileged homes.

Before there were mobile phones, you woke up in the morning to the hell-raising din of a round alarm clock. With no volume control, you silenced it with a whack on its head.

Before mobile phones, you had a music system. A multi-stack with a CD player, cassette player, radio and EQ faders. You got back from the Gulf with a red two-in-one to appreciate Mohammed Rafi and Boney M.

Before mobile phones, you went to a theatre to watch a movie. People dressed up to go to the cinema. Watching at home was a significant leap. If you couldn't afford a VCR you bought a VCP. The well heeled bought DVD players.

If you were creative, you taught yourself the camera. You thought about lenses. You figured out shutter speed and aperture. The rich bought video cameras. People dressed up to be in front of the camera. All before there were mobile phones.

Before mobile phones, random people stopped you on the road. They gestured to your watch and asked for the time.

Before mobile phones, some say, there used to be reading and writing. Not watching and texting.

I was among the first few people in India to use a mobile phone. I helped in the launch of the first mobile service in Mumbai. The service is now known as Vi. I got to handle a Motorola 'brick' with a pull-out aerial. My art partner and I made frequent calls to each other to impress family and friends.

Exciting technology. Heady times.

We thought—wow!—we'd make people talk on the move. What we didn't know was we'd also destroy old ways of life forever.

We didn't know we'd make people listen to music, set morning alarms, watch movies and cricket, take photos and videos, send messages, read the time and weather and hold meetings—all on one small device.

The damn thing replaced a ton of household things and habits.

No more queueing at the cinema. No more struggling with photography basics. No more building CD and DVD collections. No more using a pencil to unjam jammed cassettes. No more bookshelves to build. No more STD booths. No more dressing up for a shoot. No more street-corner watch repairers. No more whacking the morning alarm.

We can't even go back if we want to. No one makes DVDs and cassette players any more.

There's no rewind button to press.

*****

The shoe shop

After years of shopping online, I had an offline, brick and mortar retail experience yesterday. The occasion: an upcoming family wedding. The requirement: shoes. The result: two mysteries.

The lights were as bright and cheerful as I remembered. Red rows of chairs touched one another with low stools in front. Reassuring, familiar stuff.

The sales guy showed up with a cool pair of bright blue shoes. I told myself to behave and asked for something sober in dark tan.

He sat on a low stool. I sat on the big chair like a pasha with a subject at my feet. He uncrinkled a tissue-wrapped shoe. It's perfect for you, he said. Pashas love flattery.

I was checking out the new shoes in the full mirror when the First Mystery unfolded.

"These shoes... you'll feel very comfortable in church," he said.

Church? What church? Why did he think I was a church goer? Was religion even guessable by sight? And what about me gave him that impression? Puzzling.

Flashback. Six months ago. Coimbatore airport.

The security guard at the entrance was one of those people born congenitally happy or his boss had just resigned. He was whistling when he took my boarding card.

He read my name out loud. "Narayan?" he said, sizing me up. "I thought you'd be Thomas or Joseph." What? This guy could label me by just looking at me? I showed him my Aadhar card. He let me in.

Back to the shoe shop.

Psyched by identical deductions that were 1,200 km apart, I asked the sales guy if he had a brother who was an airport security guard. He said no, but he had a sister working in SBI, if it helped.

I let it pass. Some mysteries in life cannot be solved.

"It's tight," I said, pointing to my pinched feet.

That's when the Second Mystery unfolded. He looked to the heavens and yelled: "Number 8!" The heavens obliged. A shoebox flew into his hands from above. I swear.

The square opening in the roof of an Indian shoe shop. Home to the Invisible Shoe Man of the Attic. It was his job to remain hidden. He located, seized and hurled down shoeboxes. And recaptured unsold shoes that were hurled back at him.

The cavity and inhabitant. Both were alive and well in this day and age.

He must be 80 years old now. Still hurling like a champion. You wouldn't find him in Canada or Croatia or Cambodia. It is probably illegal there to keep a man stranded on a high perch with no steps, ladder or light.

The Invisible Shoe Man of the Attic. Only in India. All over India. Shrouded in unfathomable mystery as to his origins and continued presence. My wife rejoined me and spotted a lovely pair of dark tan slip-ons—credit where due—and we left. In the car, she said, "Just love the look of distressed leather."

I was still breaking my head over the unsolved Religious Mystery. And said the first thing off the top of my head.

"It isn't just leather that's feeling distressed right now."

*****

Cockroach milk

Cockroach milk is good for you. Don't speed read that as coconut milk. Wait, you say. There's no such thing as cockroach milk. Cockroaches aren't mammals.

But then you don't know about the Pacific Beetle Cockroach domiciled in Hawaii. It lays no eggs. The mother feeds her young a pale-yellow liquid from her brood sac.

Some humans, relaxing in their Hawaiian shorts presumably, decided to look into the matter. Perhaps they were bored. Perhaps they didn't land a new project in spite of their 'Open to Work' banners on LinkedIn.

They discovered cockroach milk contained protein crystals and amino acids, rich in lipids not produced by us. According to the NDTV site, cockroach milk was "better than every other milk that humans have ever harvested or produced."

Wow. Was this the ultimate superfood then?

As a child, I was told the tastier coffee was the one with buffalo milk. It was contested by cow's milk supporters who invented the Kumbakonam Degree Coffee, famed even today for its use of 'pyoor' cow's milk.

In early school, they told us that Gandhiji drank goat's milk. Walking past a stray goat en route to school reminded me of him. It took a slight bending of my own mind to accommodate his unusual choice of beverage.

In later classes, our world view expanded.

Arabs, we learnt, drew milk off camels while not sitting atop them. The Eskimos, poor things, living in severe places where cows were a hallucination, drank reindeer milk. Ditto the Tibetans and yak milk.

Cleopatra famously bathed in donkey milk for a glowing complexion.

To be fair, many animals were left alone. Cats, dogs and pigs. Others were unattainable. Tigers and lions intimidated. Kangaroos hopped away. Elephants stomped. Horses kicked. Porcupines bristled. Giraffes needed ladders. And so on.

Besotted with milk, humans found the plant kingdom a new place to suffix. Thus was born coconut milk. Almond milk. Oat milk. Soy milk. Cashew milk. Peanut milk… even though none of them was a mammal.

And now this.

Drumroll, please. We are descending to the insect world. And the Hawaiian cockroach is the first promising candidate. (Thanks to my nephew Ashwin for grossing me out.)

The brood sac is tiny and its precious cargo miniscule. We need to cut open millions of cockroaches to extract a significant yield. No worries, scientists are on it. A profitable harvest is in the works.

Disgusting, you say. *Yuck*, you say. But you won't for long.

In five years or less, you'll be popping a daily pill calibrated with the right amount of cockroach milk in it. Because, oh come on, we need the proteins and stuff, dammit.

While cockroaches will grumble about claims of Hawaii being a paradise on earth highly overrated.

*****

WhatsApp Uncles

All of us know a certain type of person. Let's call him Mohan. I knew my Mohan when WhatsApp became a thing. He took to it like a duck to water.

Ten years later, he still sends me an image of flowers in a field against a rising sun with 'Good morning!' emblazoned in the sky.

Mohan doesn't repeat images. It's a new field each day. A new flower, a new sky. There is a cottage industry somewhere generating good morning images each day. And Mohan knows the owner personally.

These days, housing societies and other groups crush the soul out of Mohan by prohibiting good morning greetings.

His once free ranging habitat is now confined to one-on-one chats. And sundry senior citizen groups.

Mohan has of late upgraded his game. Instead of a plain 'Good morning,' it's 'Have a great Tuesday' or 'Happy Friday' now. Focused, day-based messaging.

He also sends me life advice by Confucius, Einstein, Mandela, et al. "This is your life and you shouldn't spend it on dull people who don't love you." It exhorts me to examine my own life and weed out dull people.

Mohan sends jokes—ending with a row of tiny yellow faces writhing in unbearable laughter. It lets me know the joke is concluded and I can laugh now.

Ten years of this. No day missed.

Yesterday, he sent something engaging. It was a newspaper's matrimonial section with one ad circled out:

Match for opinionated feminist. 30+ educated girl, short hair, piercings, works in social sector, against capitalism. Wanted handsome, well built, strictly 25-28 year old, only son with established business, bungalow/ at least 20 acre farmhouse. Should know cooking. No farters/ burpers please. Write to curbyourpatriarchy@gmail.com.

Wow. I sat up. This was different! Very non-Mohan. It raised tantalising questions.

Was it a prank? By whom? On whom? If genuine, what were the odds that an opinionated, well pierced feminist wanting a land-owning, bowel-controlling, culinary hunk would actually find the perfect boy who in turn desired an opinionated, well pierced feminist?

For the first time in ten years, I responded to Mohan. "Where did you get this?" He sent back, "It's a WhatsApp forward, boss. Enjoyed?" followed by a row of tiny faces tearing up with excessive laughter.

NDTV has since revealed it as a brother's prank on his sister. Oh well. That's that then. Private humour, private business. Whatever. Nothing to do with us. Or Mohan.

He's now gone back to what he does best: Sunrise and flowers.

Have a great Monday.

*****

Dates

A writer-filmmaker friend of mine, for all her creativity and years of accomplishment, was fond of saying, "Everyday you learn something new."

I had noticed a nifty arrangement on her work table. A short vase held a clutch of sharpened pencils and ball pens so tightly packed that they didn't keel over and stood proudly vertical with their points aimed heavenwards.

I had remarked that ball pens placed that way—tips pointing skywards—didn't write well because the ink dropped away from the tips ever so slowly over days and weeks. It must have made sense. She plucked out the ball pens and inserted them back the opposite way.

That's when she uttered her favourite words. *Everyday you learn something new.*

Last week, someone I met invited me to his shop in South Mumbai. Abdul Sattar's store sold dates. And gourmet dates at that.

I don't know about you, but I've held no strong opinions on dates. If you gave me one, I'd eat it. It would end there.

Abdul's invitation came at the right time. I'd been reading a fascinating book on early Islam: *The Heirs of the Prophet Muhammad* by Barnaby Rogerson. As with every well written book, the pages produced vivid mental images of caravans and sandstorms, Arabian steeds, camels, tents, passionate warriors, oases and palm trees… and dates.

And here I was in Abdul's store the next day. Coincidence? Arranged by Providence? Who knew?

The next hour turned out fruitful.

The brown-black Safawi dates from Saudi Arabia. The dark, rich Ajwah dates also from Saudi, specifically Medina. The melt-in-the-mouth Sukkari Ruhtab. I got a box of them for an elderly relative—after completing the due diligence of sampling one myself. And the prized Medjool dates…

I got to taste everything by the simple expedient of asking, "And what is that one, Abdul?"

The real deal, in my opinion, was pedigreed dates with fillings. Dark chocolate, cranberry, caramel, hazelnut, walnut, pistachio, almond and God knows what else were wedged inside the dates. Nuts are gifts to mankind.

It was easy to overindulge on dates as delicious as these. The packaging was top class. And I decided I'd be gifting dates to my friends and associates this Diwali. I expected my standing would go up with them.

In about an hour, I shook hands with Abdul warmly and staggered away with a succulent residue in my mouth and a few bags in hand. I felt like a date connoisseur. In the manner of folks taking a crash course online and instantly feeling like a million dollars.

Out of the blue, Thursday took an unsuspected turn for the better.

I learnt something new.

* * * * *

Jeans and tattoos

The main idea of being young is to not be like the old. The main idea of being old is to try and be young.

There was a time when the school and college lot flocked to a social media platform called Orkut. Safe from prying adults. Or so they thought.

Unfortunately, thirty-somethings and above opened accounts in Orkut too.

So, the young crowd moved over to something called Facebook.

Word reached the adults and they joined in.

You couldn't blame the young for wishing to take their game elsewhere. Of late, they have quietly moved on to Snapchat without informing anyone. They are hoping the adults will stay away.

You have to feel for the young people. Adults, who once used to monitor them, are now following them.

Modern India wants to be young. 40 is the new 20. 60 is the new 40. And so on.

A teen puts on her jeans. Her elderly auntie also puts on jeans. Her uncle wears them to office. Her granddad goes for walks in them.

Same thing with earrings and long hair (for men). Forty-plus men, with a cultural history of long-haired rishis and accessorised sadhus etched in their DNA, see no problem in either piercing or not having a hair cut.

In retaliation, the young have gone extreme. They have sought trends that are near-impossible for adults to follow.

And they've come up with a winner. Tattoos!

Of course, some grown-ups follow suit but stop short. They restrict themselves to a discreet image (or spouse's name) on the ankle or forearm.

The young sense the diffidence and go for the kill.

They surrender vast swathes of their skin's real estate to the prick of the tattoo artist—whole forearms and legs, back and chest, neck and shoulder, hip and navel. In glorious colour sometimes. Nick Krygios is their patron saint, not Roger Federer.

Try imitating that, you oldies. And the oldies have no answer. So far.

In smaller towns, I see young men scoring a similar victory by styling their hair in a way that their elders will never imitate.

It's some variation of the mushroom cut. Close shaven around the ears and suddenly a nuclear bomb explosion of hair above. It looks fairly hideous.

If you're young, you will deeply rejoice at my calling anything you do 'hideous'. For it signals to you that people of my age will never do such a thing. That is sweet news to you. And a victory.

The truth is such victories are never final. Never underestimate the power of the oldies. Just like they did with Facebook, jeans, long hair and earrings, they will catch up with the young sooner or later.

It is because the goal of folks of any age is really one and the same: to be young.

* * * * *

A facial for men

Do men go for facials? I had my first one last week. A coterie of close relatives conned me into it. "It's your son's wedding," they said.

Your face should light up the room. Try Korean style.

They preyed on my natural curiosity to try new things and my natural idiocy to agree to anything.

The tiny room had a slim cot. A machine beeped.

"Korean?" I checked.

"No, Chinese," the lady said.

"What's that blue thing?"

"My lunch box."

I lay down. She applied cold paste to my face. And left the room. Silence.

Mild panic. Would she return in 5 minutes? Half an hour? Next week? It was overly bright.

I shut my eyes. My mind ran wild and returned with a memory, not remembered before, from my third standard.

I sat next to S. I gave her a scented eraser with a big L for Lady. In return, she gifted me a bitten eraser with M for Monkey. Disappointing.

Why was this random memory cropping up now? Odd.

More beeps. The lady was back. Where my nose met my face, she poked with a pointy rod without an anaesthetic. My eyes teared up.

She pinched my nostrils tight and used a tiny spade to scrape. The seafaring tribe of the Bajau could hold their breath under water for a full 5 minutes.

I wasn't a Bajau. I was from Wadala East. I let out a muffled cry for help.

She placed gauze over my face to mildly suffocate me. She spread some cold glue. My vision blurred. I slid out my hand under the blanket and gave my phone to her. I asked her to take a photo of me.

Later, she left the room. Silence.

I remembered S's face. But her name? Suganti, Shanta, Sucharita… nothing fit.

It was possible—right now somewhere in San Jose or Saidapet—that S was leading a troubled life and talking to a friend. She recalled simpler times when a little boy gave her a Lady eraser.

She regretted she'd given him a terrible return gift. Waves of regret travelled far and reached him in a tiny room with a slim cot in Mumbai.

Was that why he was suddenly thinking of her? Were the regret waves just strong enough to carry the first letter but not the whole name? Was this how the universe worked?

A wet towel whacked my face. The lady was back. Vigorous scrubbing followed by a change of mood.

Where there was once violence and powerful torture lights, there was now kindness and gentle rubs.

The beeps stopped. The lights dimmed. I sat up. Three hours after capture, I was set free.

"You are glowing!" She smiled. On my phone I stared aghast at the photo she had taken of me in the role of an extra-terrestrial.

At the pre-wedding event, my son said, "Your nose is shining! Is the lighting here too bright? "

"Not at all," I replied. "It is my inner glow spreading outwards—a sacred duty of the father to light up this room."

Needless to say, his expression was priceless.

*****

A carrier on the car roof

You go the extra mile for those you like. Do you get positive karma in return?

A couple close to us from Belgium wanted to join us on a long road trip. What fun, we said.

What if their baggage was one too many? For their comfort, we decided to get a luggage carrier on the roof of our faux-SUV. At an auto accessories shop nearby, an assistant fixed one for us expertly.

These days being what they are, another shop assistant took phone videos of the first assistant fixing the carrier to post on social media.

The owner offered us tea and other accessories: seat covers with acupressure beads, steering covers, stereo systems, perfume dispensers, satellite gadgets, even a full-fitted driver's chair in plush leather. We declined.

These days being what they are, he pointed to the QR Code on the glass door that we could aim our phones at and give his shop a glowing Google review. We agreed.

If you are in a car accessories shop for two hours with nothing to do, your mind inevitably wanders. It drifts to the bleak, rainy weather outside. People with umbrellas scurry past. And then it says: You ass, what if it rains along the way? Won't the luggage on the roof of the car get messed up?

Tarpaulin. We needed tarpaulin. The owner suggested we try a hardware store and vaguely waved his hand in a non-specific direction.

My wife quickly used her phone to order a tarpaulin sheet and multi-coloured, luggage-rack straps from Amazon for a next-day delivery.

The carrier got fixed. We thanked the guy and left feeling resourceful. We gave ourselves brownie points for the tarp and straps. Great idea, well executed, we thought. Our couple would be pleased.

The logistics of how to use the tarp and straps with the luggage remained. The couple were both Ph.D's so probably useless in practical crafts like fixing luggage to roof carriers. I asked them to reach our place early at 8 am on travel day to figure things out and still make good time.

They came at 9.15 am.

I had already packed our own luggage in the boot to save time. I placed the tarp and straps on the roof in readiness. The male Ph.D surveyed the scene.

And then.

He pulled out our carefully stashed bags from the boot. In no time, he miraculously rearranged everything—their luggage as well as ours—to make them all fit within the boot somehow. Amazing. Everyone clapped.

From the empty roof, the colourful straps now stared at me aimlessly. The pointless new tarp sat limply on the useless new carrier.

In a final flourish, the male Ph.D gathered the tarp and straps off the roof. He shoved them in the gaps between bags and things in the boot. All set, he said. Let's go!

These days, it took so little to go plummeting from being positive and resourceful to feeling useless and vaguely pissed off.

*****

Probiotics

Probiotics were good, said the family doctor. For the gut, our second brain. And, by extension, for the main brain on top.

He prescribed Enterogermina two weeks ago. Every day, I've been breaking open the plastic tab of a nicely labelled vial. The packaging is premium—to probably compensate for the fact that it looks like water, tastes like water and is expensive.

I think my gut improved and, by extension, my main brain. Each morning, I happily burst into song. An old Carnatic song at that.

Entharo mahanubhavulu

Aandariki vandanamulu…

(The world has seen so many great people

Salutations to them all…)

It was a lovely song from my childhood when music like that hovered in the background whether you cared for it or not. I recalled the lyrics surprisingly well even though I didn't know Telugu.

Entharo mahanubhavulu…

A fond, older relative once pointed to the first few lines and said, just look at the humility of the great composer Thyagaraja. A friend at work said that all great Carnatic music was written by Telugus and sung by Tamils.

That set off other memories. How a group-singing Thyagaraja festival was held unfailingly near Thanjavur every year. How M.S.Subbulakshmi and other stars sang with hundreds of regular people in hair-raising unison. How there was no separation of performer and audience, everyone sat all around.

I was drowning in nostalgia. I sang along with MSS on YouTube. *Entharo…*

Yesterday, I opened a new pack of the probiotic. I instantly understood what was going on! The pack read Enterogermina or, put simply, Entero-something. And Thyagaraja, 150 years ago, sang Entharo-something.

Entero. Entharo. That accidental similarity in sound was sufficient for my trigger-happy brain to trip out in an unknown-to-me, pre-conscious way. No wonder I was shredding Carnatic music every morning without fear or favour.

When I called up a brainy friend to share this realisation, he fell silent for a beat. No doubt, he was thinking that our brains were amazing creations that rapidly plumbed the depths of memory on the flimsiest of stimuli.

Perhaps, he was impressed with the perceptive discovery I'd made upon reading the pack afresh that morning. Or, maybe, moved that my knowledge of Carnatic music was surprisingly nontrivial. I'd have taken any of that.

He did nothing of the sort."Why do the weirdest of things happen only to you?" He wanted to know. He was proving to be the kind of friend good people warn you about.

Let's get our laser focus back to what we were discussing: the efficacy of probiotics. All told, my doctor was right about the benefits including retrieving super nostalgic stuff he knew nothing about.

And we'll leave it there.

*****

The rubber stamp

In today's slick world of UPI payments, phone banking and online tax remittance, have you tried buying a lowly rubber stamp?

That little device with reverse letters set in relief. It is not a hot-selling item. It is not on anyone's shopping list. Where you can get one, no one knows.

Useless as a saucer without a cup or an idli without chutney or an old movie without Mumtaz—you get the idea—the humble rubber stamp needs an ink pad for its existential completion to make ever-lasting indigo marks on your fingers.

Like you'd voted for all party members instead of a single candidate. Where did you even go to find the low-tech pair of a rubber stamp and ink pad in today's markets?

My finance friend and expert, who suggested I consolidate my shenanigans under one single company, left out this key detail.

I was and am still into various things like creative consultancy, website building, publishing, homestay rentals and other stuff. He called them "multiple streams of income."

I liked the term. It made the things I did seem less scattershot, more deliberate.

Yet.

He omitted the serious detail of where to get a rubber stamp that our government wanted me to have. "Google it," he said.

Google told me there was a rubber stamp maker in my locality opposite ICICI bank. I parked in front of the bank and crossed the road.

I found a textile shop, a shoe shop, a provision store, an ATM, a couple of flower shops… but no rubber stamp maker.

After walking to and fro a couple of times, the smell of freshly made popcorn hit me. I took shelter there. I hadn't eaten popcorn in ages. I crunched away by the side of the main road and mused on rubber stamps and life in general.

I gazed at Google's landmark bank opposite and at the shops around me. I asked the popcorn guy if there used to be a rubber stamp maker here.

He asked me what kind of stamp I was looking for. The circular one or the rectangular one? Or the one that didn't need an ink pad? What kind of a company was I running?

He thrust a blank paper at me and asked me to write down the details I wanted etched on the stamp. The penny dropped. The popcorn maker was also the rubber stamp maker.

"So you're a rubber stamp maker too?" I smiled.

"What to do? You have to make a living any which way. That flower shop there is also mine." He smiled as I bought a dozen more packets of popcorn to take home.

I now knew exactly who he was. He was making a living not by doing a single thing but many things simultaneously. He and I were related, in a way, via that fancy phrase my finance friend had used.

Multiple streams of income, of course.

*****

Pande's phone

Clint Eastwood holds a gun to the baddie's head. Neither knows for sure if there's a bullet in the gun. Clint utters the iconic line:

"You have to ask yourself one question: Do I feel lucky today?"

The baddie surrenders.

We all have lucky days. And unlucky days (like the baddie above who, after surrender, finds out there was no bullet in the gun.)

Yesterday, the car showroom sent a man to pick up my Kia Seltos for servicing. Pande rang my bell at 9 am sharp.

He took photos of my car. "Any issues?"

I told him about the stuff that was bothering me. "I want to stop that ting-ting-ting sound when I cross 120 km per hour on highways."

"No," he said. "Can't do that for your own safety." He left with my car.

But he rang my bell soon. "Left my phone here. Can you dial my number please?" He prowled my living room with keen eyes, a jerky head and an arched back like a furtive cat. Silence.

He dragged me to the car park. He prowled between pillars. He climbed on all fours onto the back seat of my car and sniffed. No ring tone. Silence.

On my third try, a man answered. Pande ran to me gratefully, paws extended to grab my phone. "Where are you, brother?"

A man replied, "CG Building, Ali Road." Ali Road was just outside. But CG Building?

Pande couldn't obviously reach the Man's location without my phone's help. Oh well, I decided. "Let's go," I said to him. We got into my car.

At the main gate, Pande asked the security guy for directions and put the Man on speaker phone. "CG Building, ask anyone," crackled the Man.

"Scheejee," murmured the security man, looking left and right inconclusively. "CG," suggested Pande.

"Scheejee," garbled the Man on the phone.

"Shreejee," interpreted a random passerby who joined us and pointed left.

We headed left. Was Pande feeling lucky today?

We found the Man near Shreejee Building. Pande got his phone back.

It turned out the Man was an off-duty traffic cop whose pal, a coconut seller, picked the phone off the road and handed it over. "Go thank him," said the cop.

On the wrong side of the road, the seller was beheading a coconut. "Oy," yelled Pande and held up his phone.

Both waved, head-bobbed and laughed. Nothing said, everything understood. A bus driver behind kneaded his red rubber horn into squealing. We drove home to drop me off.

Given all the various people and happenstances it took to regain his phone, today was indeed Pande's lucky day!

He called it kismet. "My kismet is good. So, I get a fine customer like you and my phone comes back." He did a namaste. "About the sound… "

"Yes?"

"Play music loudly. You won't hear the ting-ting then."

In a few weeks, if you see a Seltos on NH4 racing by and playing crazy-loud Fleetwood Mac, wave out to me.

And I'll wish you a lucky day.

*****

Butter and books

My aunt always said: Man proposes, God disposes.

She appreciated the meaning. She believed the ultimate outcome of our plans is not in our hands. It is decided by a higher power. Whenever plans failed, she'd toss out the proverb.

As a newly married couple, once on a Sunday morning, my wife and me had run out of butter. I was to go and get some. That was the proposed plan.

I drove to the regular shop in IV Block but stopped to look at the notice board near the entrance. People put up little stickers on the board asking for a maid, selling a pet, announcing a garage sale, etc. It was always interesting to find out what was going on in the neighbourhood.

Someone was selling a pair of Bose speakers with a Nakamichi cassette deck—high-end stuff at a good price. Those were quality brand names worthy of worship in those days.

I realised my humble Philips two-in-one could now be replaced with classy stuff. It felt like the heavens above were sending me a personal message via a notice board in Vishal Stores. Was God himself proposing a new plan for my musical pleasures?

Speed was of the essence. The seller's house was one lane behind the shop. I got there in two minutes.

He was an audiophile like me. He was moving on to the next big thing and wanted to junk this.

He gave me a demo. We listened to Cream and Grateful Dead. We discussed Bose speakers. He touched the buttons with care. He wound up the connecting wires with nothing short of reverence. It felt good buying stuff from fellow worshippers.

An hour later, he helped me pack the speakers and the deck into my Maruti. He also came home with me to collect the cash (oh, those days before GPay.)

When my wife opened the door, she saw my new friend and me holding speakers. We went back to retrieve more stuff from the car. She saw me counting cash in the bedroom.

Once he left, my wife said, "Where's the butter?"

Long story short, we sat down and swallowed as many dry toasts as we could—in silence. Our original, simple plan had failed. I remembered my aunt's voice: Man proposes, God disposes.

Something similar happened last year at the annual Lahore Book Fair with thousands of books on display. Book lovers turned up with a plan: to buy a book or two and improve their minds.

What really happened was this. The focus on literature got distracted by food stalls. Attendees bought over 1,200 shawarmas, 800 plates of biryani and 1,600 chicken sandwiches.

What about the books? About 35 books were sold overall. Plan all you want, my aunt would have said.

But, remember, you don't get to decide what actually happens.

*****

Quora

For all the science and magic behind social media, algorithms do get it wrong.

Two years ago, I got a mail from Quora with the subject line: Can you answer this question?

It sounded important. My initial response was to see how I could help.

The question: What was pre-stressed concrete?

I'm no engineer or contractor or mason. But people who know me will tell you I'm not short of answers. I have explanations. I hold opinions. I have courage and conviction borne of the moment, not necessarily rooted in real knowledge.

But concrete? I was stumped. We all had our limits. To my credit, though, I went to the site with my answer.

"Sometimes, concrete is already worried before anything happens to it. We call it pre-stressed."

Ten days later, Quora mailed me: What was the most effective method of curing a concrete slab?

This was easy. "It depends on what it is suffering from."

The Quora algorithm was pleased to identify a genuine concrete expert. It threw me another question a week later: Did concrete ever stop curing?

This was amazing. A couple of weeks ago, it was stressed. Last week, it needed curing. And now, it couldn't stop healing itself. Concrete was turning out to be a fascinating subject.

In the weeks to follow more questions came flying in from Quora. How thick should a concrete driveway be? In M20 concrete, what was the meaning of M? What happened if you put weight on concrete that had not cured completely?

And then the basic, existential question: What was concrete?

I got tired of answering—unless something interesting came up. Like, what happened if sugar was mixed with concrete? I knew I had to answer that.

"It's the best way to build yourself a home sweet home."

The surprising bit was after the initial fooling around, I got curious and started following threads. I discovered real answers.

How did you calculate the water-cement ratio for concrete? I knew now. Did a car battery drain when placed on concrete? I knew now. Why was extra water needed for concrete? I knew now.

As well as: How would you drop a raw egg onto a concrete floor without cracking it? Someone's memorable answer was: "Just drop it, nothing will happen to concrete. Trust me, I'm an engineer."

It's been a while now. Quora has stopped sending me mail for months—it must have figured out I am a fraud.

Today, after a long silence, my inbox pinged and a familiar mail popped up.

Quora, my friendly questioner, was back in my life asking for help: How could sulphur-based concrete benefit construction projects on the Moon compared to traditional concrete?

I realised it was an important message. Not from Quora, but from the universe. A sure-fire signal to tell me what I should write about right now.

In concrete terms.

*****

The last word

There are those who must have the last word. Always. Even in a WhatsApp chat, they have to type the last words and exit.

You send them a message: "Mailed you the invoice."

And they reply: "Will check." If you stop here, they stop.

But if you respond with "Thanks," they prolong the chat.

They type something obvious. "It's for October no?"

"Yes."

They can now have the last word.

"Thought so." And they exit.

Last Worders are often the same folks who write emails with a single word: "ok."

I was in my manager's room years ago. He was a Last Worder. His secretary came in to say that many would not be turning up for work due to heavy rains. She turned to leave the room with a casual afterthought: "Wadala is flooded."

He called her back. "Bandra is flooded. So is Jogeshwari," he boomed. "Oh," she said. She wasn't aware of those suburbs being flooded too. He nodded and added with finality, "Also Santacruz."

It seemed to me, with his body language and all, he was really saying, YOU are giving me news, lady? Please. Let ME give you the real score.

It was not just at work.

Years ago, while on a driving holiday with friends in Spain, some of us noticed a spectacular moon, low on the horizon. It looked huge and gorgeous. But we soon lost it among the trees and buildings. We gasped and went gaga. "How beautiful. Total *paisa vasool*," we said.

My Last Worder friend, who was driving, was the only one who missed it. But not one to be down for long, he waited patiently till we finished our *oohs* and *aahs*.

He then said, " I saw it first, before you all."

Wha-at? Since when did moon watching become a competitive sport?

Why did he not mention it earlier then, we challenged. "Oh, come on," he said. "It's just the moon, for God's sake. We have it in India too. What's the big deal about seeing the moon? Sheesh."

We seethed in silence. While he basked quietly in his final word superiority. Last Worders play to win.

Is it fun being a Last Worder? Maybe yes. I tried recently to be one and find out. I needed a digital specialist. I interviewed a candidate via online chat. On a whim, I decided to be a Last Worder.

When she said, "Thanks for your time," I concluded with, "No problem. We'll let you know. Cheers."

But she pressed on. "It means a lot to me." Hey, this is my interview lair. I get to have the last word and closure. "Sure, bye then," I said.

She persisted. "Have a great weekend."

We Last Worders don't give up. "You too," I insisted.

She veered away from words altogether and sent me a thumbs up emoji. Now what? I shot back a namaste emoji. Exit.

Since then, I turned into a Last Worder. In chats, emails, comments, DMs and in person. Kinda fun but you can't always beat bigger, better pros doing it for years.

Some days I'm the bug, other days I'm the windshield.

* * * * *

A boat for hire

It's not often you stand on a windy pier in busy Mumbai and stare at the blue ocean. I was there to hire a boat for my son's wedding reception.

This was a strange part of the city: a world of wharves, brokers and agents, extra thick ropes, ferries and bobbing sail boats tied to capstans. And a strong smell of fish.

A crow flying away from here reached Oman. A crow with stamina, that is.

"Office number 3?" I asked around. A man pointed to the white wall with a metallic gleam at waist level that was a door handle.

I entered a room as wide as my shoulders. If I'd fallen face first, my head would have touched the far end.

Inside, there was a desk and a man somehow squeezed behind.

"Majid," he said.

"Show me some boats," I said.

Majid? Some 500 years ago, an Omani named Majid was the best mariner of the age. The great Vasco da Gama was floundering in self-doubt on the eastern shores of Africa, unsure how to tame the monsoon winds to get to India.

By sheer luck, the two men met and hit it off. Majid the genius steered Vasco's fleet safely to Kozhikode, making him the first European to reach India by sea.

The local leader, the *Samoothiri*—who had the sea for a border—became the Zamorin in Portuguese.

Today's Majid showed me an album of boat photos. With bright decorations, bright pink balloons, bright festoons, etc.

"Garish," I told my son Tejas on the phone in a neutral voice so that Majid wouldn't catch on.

"Put up your own decorations," said Majid, who did catch on. Tejas advised me, "Whatever you do, avoid a boat with a green floor."

Why? "Because we don't want a ferry. We want a boat." I re-checked the photos. They all had green floors. I asked to see quality boats.

The Portuguese were master ship builders, ahead of the Dutch, French and English. Their caravels and carracks were built for speed. Once they learnt the ropes from Majid on the maiden voyage, they returned on their own.

They patrolled the west coast from Cochin to Cambay in search of the '5 glorious spices' of the Indies: pepper, cardamom, cloves, nutmeg and mace.

They didn't need Majid any more. Life had moved on.

In the squished room, Majid showed sleek, new boats. Tejas approved one. "What about alcohol, then? Would you arrange? Or should we?"

Majid's face fell. "No alcohol at sea," he said. "Banned."

"Oh," Tejas and I sighed together.

"Yes," said Majid, "Check Google. Sorry."

No alcohol for a Mumbai crowd? Plans for an oceanic reception went pffft.

When they first met, da Gama got Majid drunk so as to make him agree to pilot the trip. If not for that, there would have been no Portuguese voyages, no history book mentions, no Goa as we know it, no Vasco the great.

500 years on, history repeated itself in my neck of the woods. No booze, no boat. I shook hands. Get back to you later, Majid. Unlike the Portuguese, I never returned.

I didn't need Majid any more. Life had moved on.

*****

Coffee and ice cream

Why would anyone lick an ice cream cone in bone numbing cold? But that's what I saw. A kid eating ice cream with winter winds still blowing in Europe.

I grew up in the searing heat of Chennai. My parents warned us about eating ice cream in any season. "You'll catch a cold," they said.

And here was this little girl sitting on a windy bench off Lake Constance, so absorbed in her ice cream.

Other people drifted by eating ice cream. A tiny parlour nearby did brisk business.

And here we were, a couple of visitors from India, clutching our fleece jackets and still managing a shiver. With ice creams being the farthest thing on our minds.

"Would you like some ice cream?" asked our hosts earnestly. Perish the thought, we said to ourselves.

It was not a restricted, local thing. Over the next five days of a car trip across six countries—Belgium, Germany, Switzerland, France, Liechtenstein and Luxembourg—we saw people in open-air cafes eating ice creams and drinking Cokes with lots of ice. While still in their woollen caps and warm jackets.

I remembered in the US and UK too, paper cups were first filled up with tons of ice cubes before the beverage splashed down to fill in the gaps.

A friend's voice from long ago resounded in memory: There's no feeling like enjoying an ice cream, boss, in wintry Delhi.

It's been a strange sight to me to observe people in cold places eating and drinking cold things. Of course, they relish their coffee, tea and hot chocolate as well. But the popular preference for cold stuff is puzzling.

It shouldn't be, really.

Look at India. For a hot country, we eat and drink a lot of hot stuff. No one likes a cold meal. Everyone wants it piping hot.

We relish our hot teas and hot coffees. Not to mention hot samosas and steaming idlis. Of course, we enjoy our soft drinks, *nimbu paani* and ice creams.

But we thrive on our hot stuff. We can't begin our day without scalding hot chai or coffee.

Why do we do this? Is the heat around us not oppressive enough? Where does the need to gobble hot things come from?

Why hot countries enjoy hot stuff and cold countries enjoy cold stuff is a mystery. Shouldn't it be the opposite? Always and without exception?

Lost in thought, I take a satisfying sip of my hot morning cuppa here in sultry Mumbai.

*****

New stuff

For centuries, a minority invented stuff. Like the bulb, telegraph, telephone, radio, TV, trains, coffee and tea, computers, cell phones, IPL, ChatGPT…

The majority narrowed its eyes with suspicion.

In 1825, when trains were new, the Wall Street Journal said speeds like 30 miles per hour could kill. Limbs would be torn. Uteruses would fly out.

People worried about the telephone saying it would make society lazy and anti-social. (Some said it would be used, horror of horrors, to communicate with the dead.)

In the late 1800s, Spectator magazine suggested that the 'poetry of the English language' would be ruined by the telegraph with its 'conversational abbreviations.' Just like today's purists worry about SMS chat with its lol, btw and 'osum' for 'awesome.'

Many believed TV would hurt conversation, reading and the patterns of family living. It would vulgarise society.

My parents decided not to buy a TV because it would badly affect my studies. (I watched everything on my neighbour's TV but did not flunk.)

Editorial voices in Chennai thundered against the new coffee habit in the 1920s: "a degenerate innovation at which the older generation shake their heads."

Many of us thought computers at home were harmful. Today's parents believe virtual reality blurs the lines between fact and fiction. Young people will live out their violent fantasies.

It's the same story, isn't it?

The majority doesn't like new. Small marginal steps are fine—like colour TV over black and white TV or electric idli grinders over stone ones. Those are all good and nice.

But big, life-changing inventions? No way, say the majority. We want continuity, comfort, predictability… don't trouble us with new ideas, please. Go away.

How, then, did all the inventions above become realities? What brought about change? What overcame resistance?

Young people, I think. As much as the old want to keep the status quo, the young want change. It's in their blood.

In every era, the young give us our rightful share of new. And they hankered for Pink Floyd, Prince of Persia, answering machines and ODIs. Today, they cry for BTS, Legend of Mushroom, ChatGPT, virtual reality immersion, and T20.

Save us from sameness, they wail. *Save us from boredom. Save us from older folks.* Country by country, region by region, home by home, the young usher in real change outside of newspapers and TV.

That is why when your daughter sidles up to you with a winning smile today, you never know what you are being primed for.

And what new future is being plotted under your very nose.

*****

6

Then

If the past were different

IT WOULD'VE BEEN nice to have had mobile phones in earlier times. When I played cricket for my school, there was this boy who played cricket for his school: K.Srikkanth.

Yes, the same boy who went about his swashbuckling ways to play for India and was part of the World Cup winning team.

We played for the same team later at junior college level. I was the keeper and he was first slip. We weren't thick friends, but shared an occasional joke. A year later, I went on to a regular college and he got into engineering, so we played against each other.

In a memorable match (for me), he fell early to a rising ball that caught the shoulder of his bat and landed in my gloves. His was a prize wicket even then and my college captain came running happily towards me.

(The practice of high-fives at the fall of a wicket was a later development, started by the exuberant West Indians. We just moped around and got on with the game. Go watch great cricketers like Bedi or Underwood taking a wicket in a Test match on YouTube. Nothing much happens. There is a vague air of embarrassment if anything.)

I could go on with more details like these. But you get the point: I used to play cricket with Krishnamachari Srikkanth.

Years later, when he had retired from the game, I saw him in the car park of an airport—Bengaluru, maybe, it was.

I told him of our school playing days and the later college days. He did not remember.

I told him I used to be known by certain initials. I was the keeper. I even named a college-level fast bowler whom he once hit disdainfully for three consecutive sixes. He was polite but clearly, he had no clue who I was.

Since I had a big memory for trivial detail, I told him we had once sat down on rolled matting in the college pavilion after a game and smoked cigarettes that he said were from Nigeria. The brand name was Kali.

He smiled but didn't remember.

There was nothing much to do after that except to shake hands, wish each other well and walk off. It was clear that in the time after college that I went on to meet a thousand new people in my life, he went on to hobnob with a million new people.

So, the point is this.

If only.

If only there had been cellphones in our young days, my exulting captain who came running at me from cover may have taken a photo of his keeper still holding the ball aloft in his gloves. He may have even taken a photo of a dejected Cheeka departing the field with drooping shoulders.

Years later, at the airport carpark, I could've flashed these photos to Srikkanth on my phone as a telling reminder. You remember me now? Do I seem familiar now?

He could have said, "Oh, yes. Of course! How are you, man?" Or, he could have said, "That was you? You look so different!"

Either way, we could have taken it from there.

Oh, well.

* * * * *

A lake with a lesson

Many lessons in early life are learned not by gentle instruction, but by a swift kick to the backside.

To cool off from the hot sun of our summer holidays, my friends and I—a gaggle of boys aged nine or ten—visited a lake beneath a bridge in the quiet part of the city. Two of us couldn't swim. Me and another chap.

It was a lonely, isolated place. Stray buffaloes looked at us with suspicion. We jumped into the cold water with whoops and yells after leaving our clothes and footwear in a heap on a dry spot.

I stood in waist deep water. Once stable and confident, I splashed water at others.

The other non-swimmer in the group stayed on the shore. He was nominated the minder of our clothes.

It was in the nature of things that no one could be a passive minder of clothes for too long. Especially when everyone else was having fun.

With a loud shout to draw attention to himself, the minder raised his arms over his head and jumped into the water. He went right in and for a few seconds remained in.

The better swimmers yanked him out and I still remember the bemused expression of the minder as he surfaced, as if he didn't expect the medium of water to be this fluid and treacherous.

With all the joyous shouting and splashing, no one noticed that someone had stolen our clothes on the shore.

We rushed out of the water and saw an urchin boy in the distance, walking away with our clothes. Not running, but walking away. He in fact looked back at us and slowed down, as though he wanted us to catch up with him.

Through a pathway between trees, we ran after him. He laid the heap at the foot of a big tree.

A long-haired adult sat on a concrete bench built all around the tree, like in a panchayat scene in the movies. He smoked a *beedi* and sat cross-legged.

He motioned us to sit down.

Wet bottoms hit dry sand. His speech was brief. He pointed to some buildings along the edge of the water and asked us if we knew what those were.

We didn't. Those were sections of a veterinary hospital, he said. All sorts of medicines and waste and chemicals were let out into the lake everyday from there.

"You see those buffaloes? They are washed in the same water you were swimming in. You will fall sick if you come here. Very sick. If I ever see you here again, I will drown you all."

He flicked the last bit of the *beedi* away, for it had become too small and hot to hold.

We grabbed our clothes and ran.

If you're a head honcho somewhere, the point is this: if you have to make a threat, do it calmly, state the facts and consequences. And keep it short.

The lesson went deep inside us, for we never returned to that general neighbourhood for years.

*****

The explainer of English movies

When we were young, my friends in the middle-class locality I grew up in bestowed on me the unofficial title of "Explainer of English Movies."

I would explain the conversational bits they couldn't follow. I enjoyed playing the superior person.

The truth was that for every 100 English words I knew, they knew 10. With that overwhelming ratio, I was easily the one-eyed king in the land of the blind.

My good friend and neighbour, Ram, didn't like English movies that weren't cartoons or Charlie Chaplin. I persuaded him to come and see *Jaws* with me.

I promised him wondrous, unmissable special effects that everyone was talking about. Plus, I was always there to explain the complicated bits.

There is a scene from the movie that has stayed with me—even though it's not the most dramatic or a scary special effect.

It's when an elderly lady stepped onto the boat and slapped one of the main heroes. She was upset because her husband had been devoured by a shark and these heroes had done nothing to prevent it.

The man (Roy Scheider, I think) took the slap stoically, strong and silent. In Tamil or Hindi films, a slap was always returned with a slap and more.

So, my issue was this: why didn't the hero react? Retaliate, boss. Do something. It was not your fault. It was the damned shark that ate your husband, lady. Why are you letting the poor guy have it? Unfair, unfair.

As we walked out in silence after the movie, heads bowed, I was still thinking about that scene.

Ram was looking very happy. All the departing patrons were looking happy too—they'd got their full *paisa vasool* from the classic shark story ever.

"So, how was the movie?" I asked Ram.

"You remember when that lady slapped the man on the boat?" he replied.

Of all the fascinating things in the movie, this was a surprising little detail for Ram to talk about. I remembered it, of course.

And Ram said, "What responsibility, man!"

What? I didn't quite understand what he was talking about. What responsibility? Whose responsibility? I was frankly surprised that Ram—a far simpler guy than me—even knew a big English word like 'responsibility.'

It turned out that he answered the same question that had bothered me too. Why did the hero not react?

The hero took the blow silently because it was his job to stop the shark attacks and he had failed. The hero had taken responsibility for his failure to protect. And my friend was rightly impressed with that strength of character.

Ram got it. And he was now explaining the nuance to the Explainer! Mr Spielberg had gone over my head and somehow reached out directly to Ram to make his point.

My respect for Ram went up so much that I paid for both our bus tickets on the way home. For the rest of the evening, the Explainer of English Movies resigned from his role.

And had a normal, two-way chat about the movie.

* * * * *

The TV quiz show

Long before quiz stalwarts like Derek O'Brien and Siddharth Ray, there was a TV quiz show I still remember.

The quiz master was all high energy. A dozen contestants stood meek and rigid in three rows. There was no Team A or B or C.

Just one big cluster of deer caught in the headlights. They were chosen for the show, apparently, by roping in people who were passing by the Chennai TV studio.

All were men. They wore the dark-hued, handloom shirts handed out by the studio. The video cameras in those days couldn't handle the extreme contrast levels of overly bright clothes.

The quiz master boomed. "What is the German Shepherd dog more popularly known as?"

No one said a word. Watching at home, a clever friend among us knew the answer: "Alsatian!"

Great. We could all enjoy this now, not with a tense air of suspense but an air of superiority instead.

The quiz master boomed the question again. No answer. We were giggling already.

Then he began to take the question apart in detail for everyone's benefit.

"There is this dog, right? I'm talking about its breed. German Shepherd. But we all know the breed by a different name. A very common name. What is it?"

No answer.

The quiz master prowled about, managing the long trailing mic cord behind him expertly. He boomed again.

"See, there is this dog that is technically known as the German Shepherd. But it is popularly known by another name. Can you tell me the popular name?"

A man in the back row wearing the Government-issued handloom shirt, ventured: "Jimmy?"

Almost every dog in the city—those in homes and those loosely attached to tea shops—was called Jimmy then. It was a popular name alright.

We lost it. One of my friends rolled off the sofa and writhed on the mosaic in what became abbreviated later to ROFL.

I've thought about that contestant a lot. It's easy to see his predicament in retrospect.

He must have 'known' the answer even when the question was thrown the first time.

But like with all of us, there must have been a restraining inner voice telling him to shut up. *Don't make an ass of yourself. Keep quiet.*

But then the quiz master asked the question again and again. The resolve melted with repeated taunts.

The inner voice changed its tune: *Go for glory, brother. You'll regret it later if you keep silent.* Thusly, he moved from total self-doubt to total confidence.

The gung-ho ring master, of course, rejected his answer. The contestant slunk back and never said a word again.

For all the laughing we did as kids, future life gave us enough situations like this—to feel self-doubt first and then self-confidence in turn, not knowing which one to trust and not always turning out victorious.

If life is a quiz, we don't always have the answers. The best response is to laugh heartily as we used to long ago.

Except, this time, at ourselves.

* * * * *

An imposter at a wedding

Some years ago, at a family wedding in faraway, fancy London, I got mistaken for something I'm not. By the elderly grandmother of the groom.

It happened at a pre-wedding meeting between the families. My wife and me were on the bride's side. I was placed next to the groom, while my wife was assigned to chat with the said grandmother of the groom.

A gentle, frail and gracious lady, full of life and loved by all.

The groom next to me was an easy conversationalist. He handled small talk well, always a good thing. I noticed my wife and *Dadi-ji* across the room chatting pleasantly.

I knew they were talking about me from the way the grandmother glanced at me often. As they were about to leave, she approached me and said, "I respect poets."

Turning to her grandson—the groom—she said, "He writes poetry. Do you know how much brains it takes?"

The groom looked at me surprised. "You are a poet? Wow, I didn't know that."

I was simultaneously wondering how to refute this while being curious about what exactly my wife had told her.

I'd written advertising jingles for countless brands but it was difficult to classify those as poetry. In the hubbub of overlapping goodbyes of a lot of people, the moment just passed and I ended up saying nothing.

I later checked with my wife. Unsure if the grand old lady would understand what a copywriter was, my wife generalised me as a writer and the lady was promptly impressed.

At what point the 'writer' got upgraded to a 'poet' we would never know.

"It must be your long hair," my wife suggested.

At the grand reception on wedding day, *Dadi-ji* walked up to us with her ever-present smile. She introduced us to someone who was the mayor of a London suburb (or district or whatever.) And she introduced me as a 'director.'

Wha-at? Surely, this wasn't happening. (It turned out my wife had used the term 'creative director.')

That gentleman handed me his visiting card and penned his private mobile number at the back.

If ever I needed someone to play the part of a judge, he said, I could call on him. I explained that I wrote scripts for short advertising films, but was not a Bollywood film director.

However, people believed what they chose to believe. He nodded vaguely but continued to talk about being a qualified lawyer who could do justice to a judge's role. He explained his rise to the mayor's office from humble beginnings in Ludhiana.

Twice within a couple of days, I found myself pretending to be someone I was not. This was no imposter syndrome. I was a plain imposter, period.

Some are born imposters. Some achieve it in time. And some, like me, have it thrust upon them.

*****

Those good old movies

Indian movies today, even the ones with a banal script, have decent production values. The camera work is good, the scenes art directed, the acting pretty decent.

It wasn't this way.

Some decades ago, the ad industry, for instance, turned out more polished, well-crafted work than the 'mass-market' film industry.

Care and attention were devoted to producing TV commercials that barely lasted seconds. As against 3-hour marathon works for the cinema halls that came with inbuilt shoddiness—in the plot, casting and overall aesthetics.

In a typical ad shoot for a soft drink, for instance, just the lighting of a product shot would take hours.

Watching the slow progress of a TV commercial shoot, a light boy in Bengaluru was puzzled. He said, in his experience, feature films on the contrary were shot at breakneck speed.

"You people here are fussing for hours over a shot that will last 3 seconds on the TV screen… but in a film shoot they finish whole sequences in a day."

As an example, he recalled his time with a film unit shooting on location in Rajasthan. The evening light was fading fast and the shot was that of a major South hero on a high wall (or his stuntman, more likely), doing a jump onto a horse below.

In post-production, the scene was to be reversed so that the hero would appear to be first astride a horse and then rise magically through the air and land on the high wall.

With light fading fast, no one noticed (or cared) that when the stuntman jumped onto the horse, the surprised horse… shat. "I saw the tail lift and out shot a pile of shit on the sand," he concluded.

Such things happen. In all shoots of any kind, in some form or the other, as the expression goes, 'shit happens.'

I asked him "Surely, they did a re-take, right?"

"No way," said the light boy. "That's not the way they did things."

"It's playing in that theatre over there," he said, waving a hand at the street below. "Go see what they did."

Some of us did watch the movie the next evening. And it was all there, like he said. No re-takes, no nothing.

On the big screen, the hero came smiling astride the horse. Some baddies crossed his path and challenged him.

To their surprise, the hero flew up through the air and landed triumphantly on the side wall, hands akimbo and a superior smile.

And, best of all, the horse shit that lay in clumps on the sand rose and flew back into the horse's rump!

I remember looking around the hall to gauge the audience's reaction to this display of onscreen lunacy. None of the paying patrons were bothered. Random folks applauded the hero's one-upmanship.

We've come a long way since then. The movie industry has caught up on standards—in editing, lighting, sound design and even poster design.

And we have a better quality audience today whether for movies, music or on YouTube. Increasingly, and mercifully, today's audiences won't take shit.

* * * * *

Humour on demand

Some have it. Most don't. Humour of the spontaneous kind is a gift only a few lucky ones have.

All of us know someone who routinely comes up with clever things to say at a given moment.

Some years ago, I ate seriously delicious *medu vadas* and *masala dosas* at an Indian wedding in a remote London suburb. I praised the catering cook and remarked that every obscure ingredient for Indian cuisine was apparently readily available in the UK these days.

The man replied, "Barring a father and a mother, you get everything else here."

The response does not sound like much in print, but in person, it was funny. It not only answered the question but did it joyfully and unexpectedly.

Decades back, a passerby stopped my friend Rajesh on the street and asked him the way to a politician's house in the neighbourhood.

Rajesh didn't know much about the politician beyond the fact that he was tall, thin and bald. But he knew the directions and gave them.

Curious about the distance, the man asked, "*Lamba hai kya?*"

Rajesh replied, "*Haan aur takloo bhi hai!*"

(The guy asked, "Long?" And Rajesh, taking the alternate meaning of the word that meant 'tall' replied with, "Yes and bald too.")

That's a tough thing to do—on the spot, just like that.

Rajesh also employed his skill in stressful times. His scooter once conked out just as the traffic lights turned green. He kicked the starter furiously to no avail.

The car behind him honked non-stop and Rajesh lost it. He put the scooter on its stand and walked up to the car driver.

"Why don't you go to my scooter and try kick-starting it?" he suggested. "Meanwhile, I'll sit here and keep honking."

After a surprised beat of silence, the driver broke into laughter and made peace.

The late great American writer Dorothy Parker was known for her quicksilver repartees. As she went through the doorway of a fancy hotel, a leading socialite of the time approached her from the opposite direction.

The socialite, with fake deference and pure bitchiness, yielded way to Dorothy saying, "Age before beauty."

And Dorothy breezed past her, remarking, "Pearls before swine."

At the US customs, Oscar Wilde responded famously with, "I have nothing to declare except my genius."

It's not about making a joke. It's about making a point or answering a question—with grace and wit.

Feeling stressed? Find yourself people like Dorothy, Oscar or Rajesh. They have a certain something in their souls that generates spontaneity. They make our lives lighter and merrier.

Dorothy Parker said, "Wit has truth in it; wise-cracking is simply calisthenics with words."

The crazy bit about coming up with a witty and apt response is that all of us have done it—after the event has passed! Everyone thinks up the perfect response, hours or days later. Or, sometimes, years later.

A response so humorous, insightful, cutting and pertinent that it evokes lasting admiration. But alas. It comes too late and within the confines of your own mind.

Cheer up. We have all been there.

*****

Coacher

In my school days, to help us improve our cricket, we had a Coacher. Not coach. 'Coacher.'

To us kids, the word had an acceptable, spontaneous logic to it. One who swam was a swimmer; one who drove was a driver. So the one who coached was a coacher. Duh.

"Coacher told me to work on my cover drive."

"Coacher says my boots are not good quality."

The word rolled easily off our tongues.

It took a while to realise that 'coacher' never appeared in newspapers and magazines. No teacher or newsreader used it. And students from better schools looked at us like we were idiots.

'Coacher' died a natural death in a few years. The logic was sound, but no one outside our little circle endorsed it. So, we went back to the accepted convention of saying 'coach.' Not Coacher, you moron, we told one another. It's Coach.

I still have a fondness for Coacher and if we'd had social media support then, we could have campaigned for it and changed the wor(l)d.

Today, a word like 'mentee' has entered the mainstream. It was born in 1958, then presumed dead or missing for decades and today, it is back as a reigning champion.

It's everywhere on social media and very popular with the training community. It thrives on similar logic. If there is a trainer-trainee, employer-employee and so on, why not a mentor-mentee?

The lack of popular support outside of our little circle killed 'coacher'. But the massive online usage of 'mentee' has given it wings, taken it places. It must be obviously fulfilling a need that hadn't been felt for centuries.

We also hear 'coachee' as a synonym for mentee. Even though there is no 'coacher.' It's an obscure (though legit) word to use even though there are good alternatives in ward, student, protégé and pupil.

It may be a good time now to petition for the revival of 'coacher' as its matching pair.

Where next now?

Lecturee, teachee, managee, believee, givee, sellee, photographee… bring them on. Who am I to stand in the way of progress?

*****

7

North-Southﾠ

Hindi in the South

THE NORTH INDIA vs South India thing—it's been there for years. Twenty years ago, a colleague in Delhi returned from a holiday in the South and was puzzled by the Hindi, or the lack of it, there.

He said to me, "The shopkeepers understand Hindi but they won't reply. They all know Hindi there but they won't speak it."

They all knew Hindi but wouldn't speak it. Really?

A few years ago, a colleague in Mumbai visited Kerala for a 'great holiday' and made this observation: "Waiters and cab drivers understand Hindi but they won't speak it. Weird, man."

My friends weren't chauvinists, just regular people with an observation. Why did they conclude that people down South knew Hindi but were reluctant to speak it?

I grew up in Chennai. I didn't know a word of Hindi. No one we knew spoke it. Whatever Hindi we picked up was from Hindi movies. A supporting character like Ashok Kumar or Om Prakash exited a room. At the doorway, he paused, turned and uttered a single word: "Lekin."

Cut to shocked family members. He then revealed something stunning. I was the one who killed your father. Or, your mother is not your mother. Or, the rapist is in this very room now.

We had no trouble understanding from the context that 'lekin' meant 'but'. Pretty much the same scene happened in Tamil movies too.

When Amjad Khan drawled, "Arre, O Samba," we figured out the lackey in question was named Samba.

When Amitabh boasted of his bungalow, car and other goodies, we understood Shashi Kapoor's superb riposte: "Mere paas Ma hai." We got it. We were thrilled. We whistled.

When Asrani said anything, we laughed in principle because he was a funny guy. We also laughed when Dharmendra cried.

We loved our Hindi movies. They were slicker, the clothes fancier and the songs were great. But Hindi as a language? We didn't speak it. We didn't know how to and there was no desire either.

My Northern friends assumed Hindi was everywhere. How could someone be in India and not know Hindi? Not possible, no?

Given this assumption, it couldn't be that the vegetable seller in Kochi didn't know Hindi. That was unthinkable. It could only be that the man refused to speak it—for whatever perverse reason.

The real reason, folks, is simple enough.

No one speaks Hindi in interior Karnataka or Kerala or Tamil Nadu for the same reason that no one in UP speaks Spanish or Malayalam. They don't have anyone around who speaks them or needs to.

We speak what those around us speak. We may relish an Andhra pickle, wear a Kanjeevaram sari, enjoy a Goan beach and wear French perfume. But we speak what everyone around us spoke as we grew up. It's normal.

End of story.

But when I wake up tomorrow and go to Quora, there will be that guy with the same, tiresome question: Why do South Indians refuse to speak Hindi?

Time to pull my hair out.

*****

Barbers Bridge

Barbers. Also known as hairdressers. Somewhere in Madras, also known as Chennai, there is a good-sized bridge called Barbers Bridge.

Why name a bridge Barbers Bridge? Was it built to house barbers? Was Barber the surname of an obscure British official?

Turns out, in the 1700s, a water channel cut through the city. On one side lived a barber whose job was to shave a Brit engineer who lived on the other side. Every morning, he swam across the channel, shaved the sleeping sahib without waking him and swam back home.

At some point, fully exhausted and overly wet, the barber begged for a bridge across the channel to make life easier. The engineer obliged. Thus was born the Barbers Bridge.

True? No one knows.

Here's the more likely version.

A British administrator Lord Hamilton built the bridge in the 1700s and named it after himself: Hamilton Bridge. People in power did that sort of thing.

Unlike Kannada that loves names starting with 'h' (Hebbal, Hubli, Hampi, Hospet, Hassan, Haveri, Hosakote, etc.), Tamil swallows and digests the leading 'h'. So, Hamilton Bridge, to the locals, came to be known as Ambiltun Bridge. It remained that way for 100 years.

In the 1800s, a British surveyor catalogued local names of streets and bridges to standardise them in English. He came upon Ambiltun Bridge and asked his interpreter what the strange word meant.

"Barber," said the interpreter.

Why? Because 'Ambiltun' sounded pretty close to the Tamil word 'ambattan' which meant 'barber.' Many locals were already calling it Ambattan Bridge. The surveyor formally recorded the name as Barbers Bridge in his register.

The name stuck for the next 100 years—till very recently, in fact.

Hamilton Bridge → Ambiltun Bridge → Ambattan Bridge → Barbers Bridge.

In the memorable words of researcher Gauri Viswanathan, *"The metamorphosis of the distinguished Lord Hamilton, seeking posterity in bridge naming, into a commonplace barber, is one of the most delightful post-colonial rewritings of history..."*

In recent times, our politicians renamed it Dr Ambedkar Bridge to end the fun and keep all bridges dead serious.

*****

Marketing: South vs North

Is marketing to North India different from marketing to South India? Sure, people are people everywhere.

But there is this thing called 'cultural values.' A shared set of assumptions and behaviours. It feels self-evident and true to those within.

Once you cross the Vindhyas from either direction, this world of cultural values and shared assumptions shift—sometimes a little, sometimes a lot.

A North-Indian marketing professional from a couple of decades ago took our team out for a drink. He was an experienced and successful guy. Very street-wise, not an 'expert' who had read all the books.

More Sehwag than Bhogle.

His experience of dealer visits was noteworthy.

In Ludhiana in the North, for instance, he would be invited by a prominent dealer/distributor to his home. After leisurely conversation and dinner, when it was time for our man to leave, the dealer would accompany him to the front gate on the pretext of being courteous.

In reality, the dealer was there to observe what sort of company car the sales guy came in. If it was a lowly, basic-model Maruti, he concluded that this new company was heading nowhere.

It was obviously miserly, cheapskate and lacking confidence in its future to treat its sales managers so shabbily.

On the other hand, if it was an Esteem or Accent (of those days) or better, then the dealer felt comforted. The company was positive and confident of its future, always a good sign.

In a place like Salem in the deep South, however, the opposite held true. There too, a prominent dealer would call you over for dinner and later accompany you to the street with the same intent of finding out which car you came in.

If your company car was relatively posh, his heart sank. He knew instinctively this company was headed nowhere. It was obvious that this was a showy, profligate and careless company.

If yours was a humble Maruti Alto, his mind lit up. Surely, this company would go far, for it understood frugality and moderation.

Even allowing for the inevitable embellishing of detail in after-work chitchat, there seemed to be a grain of truth in what the man was saying.

Is it true today?

We've come a long way as a country in the last two decades. We're better homogenised than before due to travel, exposure and intermarriage. It's difficult to say how true this dramatic divergence in North-vs-South (culturally) holds today.

On that evening, in that dimly lit pub with the old pro holding forth, everyone getting tipsier by the minute, it certainly felt unquestionably true.

*****

Filter coffee

Ethiopia gave coffee to the world. And the decoction settled firmly in South India.

Europeans created the estates and drank the coffee—a colonial thing. No Indian touched the stuff. Plantations came up in the Mysore region at first and spread.

In the 1900's, the ruled followed the rulers, starting with the upper classes. Brahmins and Vellalars of Tamil Nadu were the early adopters. The daily habit mushroomed in quick time.

Coffee became a symbol of hospitality. R.K.Narayan went on to say that a middle-class South Indian "cannot feel that he has acquitted himself in his worldly existence properly unless he is able to ask any visitor who may drop in 'Will you have coffee?'"

Critics were quick to attack this mass movement. They called it obnoxious stuff, entering all homes and wreaking havoc. Coffee subverted the vitality of the digestive organs, they said. Even country folk who never knew this drink were taking to it in big numbers.

A historian of the time lamented:

"The old practice of taking *kanji*, or cold rice-water, in the early morning is rapidly giving way to coffee drinking, a degenerate innovation at which the older generation shake their heads."

One correspondent complained to Gandhi: "The greatest obstacle in the way of success to our non-cooperation movement are our women. They drink coffee three times a day and consider it fashionable to drink more."

There's more such anecdotal stuff in a slim book called *In Those Days, There Was No Coffee* by A. R. Venkatachalapathy. A delightful read.

My dad, for instance, bought different coffee beans and mixed them (Plantation A and Peaberry) in some magical proportion that only he knew. Every family had their own magical proportion. Some added chicory, others frowned.

Once roasted and ground, there was the actual task of making coffee. A task of precision.

The milk was added to turn "black into sepia from which emerged a brown akin to the foaming edge of a river in flood." This was serious art. Sugar was added to just cut the bitterness without producing sweetness.

I have known a family who went to 'see' a girl for their son long ago and didn't go through with it, at least in part because of the inferior coffee they were served.

The so called South Indian coffee you get in restaurants in Mumbai and Delhi falls short badly. You are drinking the name 'South Indian', not the real article. The real thing takes quality ingredients, process, patience and skill.

All available at any South Indian home, barring Kerala. There, they are acknowledged masters at tea. For some reason, they are not in love with coffee. They don't drink it or make it well. Kindly desist asking them for coffee. They don't get it.

If you travel deep into Tamil Nadu, ask for 'degree coffee' in the Kumbakonam region. It is made with unadulterated cow's milk and is top of the pops.

You may wonder if there is a Tamil word for coffee. Glad you asked.

Kaapi.

*****

When Tamil hears Malayalam

Neighbours share common words. In both France and Germany, for instance, 'bonbon' means a sweet and 'champignon' means mushroom.

If you share a common border, some words will travel back and forth with ease.

Closer home, an elephant is 'aana' in Malayalam and pretty much the same thing in Tamil - 'aanai' or 'yaanai'. An egg is 'mutta' in Malayalam, 'muttai' in Tamil.

There are many such common words.

Yet.

There are some words that sound exactly the same *but mean different things.*

'Vellam' in Malayalam means water. What you drink every day. In Tamil, 'vellam' means a flood.

To Tamil ears, someone across the border asking for 'vellam' brings forth images of disaster. Acres of agricultural land destroyed. Farmers' homes submerged. Doom and gloom.

You can rightly argue the word still means water. The difference is one of degree, not kind. It is an everyday drink in one state, breaking news in another.

Yet.

The differences can be noteworthy. The word 'kondattam' in Tamil, for instance, means celebration of a boisterous kind. Mindless dancing may be involved.

Whereas, across the border, an elderly gentleman is likely to ask his long-suffering wife to bring on some 'kondattam' to go with the evening tea.

Again, to Tamil ears, it brings to mind unseemly, wild revelry being requested of an old lady. Until you realise that 'kondattam' in Malayalam means a fried, crunchy snack—as 'chakli' in Maharashtra, 'mattri' in the North and 'murukku' in Tamil Nadu.

Same word. Totally different information. You can argue that crunchy food is a celebration of sorts for foodies but you'd be pushing it. It's difficult to make a case for why this word ended up like this.

Yet.

This can get worse. The Malayalam word 'kazhi' (with its various endings) connotes eating. The 'zh' sound, incidentally, is unique to these two languages and it's worth taking a trip to YouTube to figure out how it's pronounced.

The exact same word in Tamil, if used in polite company at all, means to excrete.

Tamil ears, yet again, feel the shock and awe of the word when it is uttered by their neighbours in casual contexts.

How did this happen? How did a word that meant stuffing your face in one language transform into a word for vacating your bowels in another?

I wonder if other neighbourly languages—Kannada and Telugu, Marathi and Gujarati, Bengali and Oriya, etc.—share common words of this kind.

I'm not talking about common words that mean the same thing in different languages. That is expected (and boring, in my opinion.)

But if there are words that sound the same but mean different things—or, preferably, wildly different things—then we are talking. That would set our minds—at least, mine—ablaze.

*****

8

Yinglish

Many states, many tongues

ENGLISH. IT'S THEIR language but we speak it our way. If you say 'skews' and 'kyoon' for 'squeeze' and 'queen', you are from Kerala.

If you say 'snakes' and 'cape' for 'snacks' and 'cap', you are from Gujarat.

If you say 'you-vur' and 'eggzyting' for 'your' and 'exciting', you are from Tamil Nadu.

If you say 'heart' for 'hurt' and 'hurt' for 'heart', you are from Bengal. (As in "I have a big heart on my knee.")

If you say 'peeen' and 'buuhs' for 'pin' and 'bus,' you are from Maharashtra.

If you say 'meyyerment' and 'klohny' for 'measurement' and 'colony', you are from Punjab.

If you say, 'unkal' for 'uncle', you are from anywhere in the North.

If you say 'yegg' for 'egg', you are from anywhere in the South.

I'm sure you can think of dozens more.

Obviously, not everyone speaks like this. But such usage is widespread to form a pattern. Stereotypes are stereotypes for a reason.

It's not just us.

If you say, "Axar is bowling wick-ut to wick-ut", you are from Sri Lanka.

If you say 'plyah' for 'player', you are from Australia.

If you say 'crick' for 'click', you are from Japan. (During the Second World War, to help the Allies tell the Japanese from friendly nationalities, the password to cross the lines was 'Lallapaloosa.' The nearest the Japanese came was 'Rarraparoosa.')

If you say 'fush' and 'chups' for 'fish' and 'chips', you are from New Zealand.

If you say 'goolie' instead of 'gully', you are Geoff Boycott.

Often, the spoken usage carries over to the written word.

A road sign in Kerala reads, "Bumb Ahead." The locals have no trouble deciphering it for an upcoming speed breaker. Written as spoken.

In neighbouring Tamil Nadu, a mysterious sign offers 'Class Danks' for sale. It's a pet shop selling glass tanks for keeping fish. Written as spoken.

A vendor with a cloth banner screaming, 'Visitable Juice' in faraway UP sells vegetable juice, of course. Written as spoken.

We shouldn't descend to the level of poking fun at simple shopkeepers struggling with a foreign language. My focus is on noticing spoken English sounds converted to written, commercial messaging.

The burning question is why. Why do we do this?

Whether in Punjab or Andhra, Bengal or Gujarat, UP or Kerala, we have our own rich, linguistic traditions of hardwired sounds. When English comes calling, we don't go out to meet it. We directly invite it into our mouth for our vernacular tongue to beat it into submission.

With colourful results.

A Sen praises Kolkata's famous 'Howrah breeze'; a Nair praises Indian math for inventing 'seero'; a Chawla praises himself as a 'karode-pati'; and a Murthy refuses praise with, "No prawlem."

I love them all. I have a digital file full of entries.

Oddly, those regions that are proud of their 'English knowledge' are the very ones with the thickest accents and blithely unaware of them.

Go figyer, as the Americans say.

*****

Kindly adjust only

It is said over 250 million people speak Indian English including the diaspora. That's a lot of people, more than the population of the UK.

Thanks to the massive worldwide following of the IPL (and its record-breaking auction prices), words like 'lakh' and 'crore' are now used routinely by sports podcasters in the UK, Australia and elsewhere.

With its quirks, innovations and local language influences, Indian English is now a well-recognised form of English internationally.

Tense:

Indian English prefers the present continuous tense over the present simple tense. Where a Brit says, "I don't understand you," an Indian is likely to say, "I'm not understanding you."

'I like your office' becomes 'I'm liking your office.' And 'Do you agree with me?' becomes 'Are you agreeing with me?'

Question tags:

You will wait for me, won't you? It doesn't work, does it? Ending phrases like 'won't you?' and 'does it?' are question tags added to regular sentences. British and American English have a variety of question tags.

We will get lost in the dark, won't we? You won't be coming to the office tomorrow, will you? I shouldn't feel bad about this defeat, should I? She's wrong in saying that, isn't she?

In Indian English, question tags are reduced to one: the single, catch-all 'isn't it?'

We will get lost in the dark, isn't it? You won't be coming to the office tomorrow, isn't it? I shouldn't feel bad about this defeat, isn't it? She's wrong in saying that, isn't it?

The words 'Also' and 'only' at the end of sentences:

Indian English places 'also' at the end of the sentence rather than before a verb. It places 'only' at the end of sentences for emphasis.

'After meeting Varsha, I will meet Shraddha also.'

'I'm going to Delhi and visiting Agra also.'

'Ankit, why are you not studying?' 'No, mom. I am studying only!'

Countable nouns:

There are countable nouns like sofa-sofas, brochure-brochures, shoe-shoes and suggestion-suggestions. And there are non-countable nouns like furniture, information, stuff and advice.

Except, in Indian English, non-countable nouns are countable. Everything is possible with furnitures, informations, stuffs, advices, etc.

All our furnitures were bought in Delhi. He gives false informations only. That shop is famous for selling bad quality stuffs. And so on.

Repeating words:

An American or Australian will invite you to his group for lunch with, "Hey, come join us." An Indian is likely to say, "Hey, come-come, join us."

Or, "I'm not a photographer-photographer. I just love shooting with my phone camera."

*****

What's your good name?

Here's some more on Indian English.

Pronunciation closely follows the spelling:

There are more silent letters in British English and American English. Take the sentence below.

Let's climb a mountain with half a sword.

The 'B' sound in 'climbs' is voiced in Indian English—the same way it is in numb, thumb, dumb, etc. So is the 'W' sound voiced in 'sword.' Although the 'L' in 'half' remains silent in all forms of English.

In odd cases, Indian English changes the spelling to match the spoken sound. The phrase 'to a great extent' is likely to be spoken by someone from Kerala as 'to a great extend.'

It then gets written as 'to a great extend', which can be perplexing if you're not from Kerala.

Inventive Indianisms:

In most types of English, 'cousin' is gender neutral. Not for us. We say 'cousin brother' and 'cousin sister' to remove all neutrality.

What is the English word for the relationship between husbands of two sisters? Fret not. Indian English from Tamil Nadu and Kerala comes to the rescue with 'co-brothers.'

Since the women are already sisters, it's good to turn their husbands into brothers. Almost.

If 'postpone' is a word, shouldn't 'prepone' also be a word?

"No way," says the rest of the English world. "Yes indeed," says Indian English. 'Prepone' now features in the venerable OED (Oxford English Dictionary). Shashi Tharoor endorses its usage.

The rest of the world enquires, "Do you eat meat?" But an Indian asks, "Do you take non-veg?" We say it without batting an eyelid—it's so obvious, *yaar*—and wonder why the world raises its puzzled eyebrows.

The world refers to 'last night' and 'this morning.' We prefer 'yesterday night' and 'today morning' instead.

Adding/dropping sounds:

Your mother tongue influences your spoken English. In Andhra Pradesh or Tamil Nadu, an initial vowel sound is added to turn 'school' into 'iskool.' Final vowel sounds are added to produce 'that-u,' 'but-u' and 'correct-u.'

In the North, vowel sounds may be dropped. A Punjabi who says 'claps' or 'klony' means 'collapse' or 'colony.'

Consonant sounds may also be added or dropped. 'Poi-yun' in Delhi means 'position' with the 's' and 't' dropped. Faraway Ernakulam is referred to by the locals as 'Erna-ulam' with the 'k' dropped.

Change of expression:

The world accepts life with, 'It is what it is.' We prefer, 'It's like that only.' The world says, 'I will be out of town.' We say, 'I will be out of station.' In Maharashtra, we also add, 'I'm going to my native.'

What the world calls a waste of time, we call 'timepass.' While the world has 'to do what's necessary,' we prefer 'to do the needful.'

If you've read this far, we share a love of language. We should shake hands. What is your good name, please?

*****

First name or last?

If you were a cricketer in the IPL, will the commentators call you by your first name or last name?

If your last name is unusual, you are set. Nobody knew of a name like Sehwag before the all-slaying opener came along.

'Virender' didn't stand a chance. 'Sehwag' won internationally.

Like, in an earlier era, commentators swooned over the magic of Prasanna, not Erapalli. Sunil didn't stand a chance. Gavaskar won.

India rejoiced in the Audi 100 awarded to Shastri, not Ravi. We applauded Dravid the wall, not Rahul the wall.

Last name domination continues. A commentator—think of Nasser Hussain or Ian Bishop in full flow—will likely say Kohli than Virat. Siraj, not Mohammed. Jadeja, never Ravindra. It pays to have a unique last name.

What if you as a cricketer don't have a unique surname? What if, alas, you are saddled with a common one like Singh, Sharma or Patel? Should you weep?

No. Your first name rules then.

They will celebrate you as Kuldeep and Rohit, not Sharma. They will glorify you as Yuvraj and Harbhajan, not Singh. Zaheer, not Khan. Axar, not Patel. Shreyas, not Iyer.

They will certainly use and popularise your full name, but helplessly revert to your first name often.

If you are a cricketer with an unusual first name, you hit the jackpot. Commentators instantly love an Ajinkya, Ruturaj, Sanju, Shikhar… how can they resist?

Unless your first name is excessively unusual like Yashasvi.

In which case the non-Indian commentators will promote you worldwide as the more pronounceable Jaiswal.

What if your name clashes with other names? If there is already a Murali Vijay and a Murali Kartik, what if you are Dinesh Karthik? They will differentiate you by your initials, DK. Not to worry.

Unlike commentators, crowds have to holler en masse. Do they pick the first or last name? Whichever is simpler.

Like the shattering din of "Dho-ni, Dho-ni" or "Koh-li, Koh-li" surname chants. Since two syllables are perfect, a Jadeja is reduced to "Jad-du, Jad-du."

Yet, we also have the full throated first name shoutouts of "Ro-hit, Ro-hit." And the nostalgic, seismic power of "Sach-iiin, Sach-in."

On rare occasions, commentators refer to a player by both names without exception.

Joe Root is always Joe Root. Kapil Dev is always Kapil Dev. (A singular exception was the late great Aussie commentator Richie Benaud, who insisted on "Dev.")

Across the border too, those who opine over microphones make instinctive, collective decisions. They talk of Afridi, not Shaheen. Rizwan, not Mohammed. But somehow Babar, not Azam.

So, play hard and win big at the auction. But get your name right for the commentators and crowds to catapult you to glory. You have our best wishes.

I know. You are deeply wondering how jobless a person must be to dish out advice like this.

I hear you.

* * * * *

Timepass

We are all immersed in a world of Indian English that we take for granted.

Here's a random selection of Indianisms from an infinite list. Some you will recognise. Others will look odd. It depends on which part of India you are from.

Kindly adjust:

You enter a crowded train and see five people sitting on a long seat meant for four. You politely request them to 'kindly adjust'. They squeeze up and make space for you. The Bengaluru version is "adjust maadi."

Have a head bath:

It's when you wet your hair and clean it in addition to your body. South India also has an "oil bath" where oil is liberally applied to the hair and body, and washed off during the bath.

Give a missed call:

You'd have no trouble understanding if I told you, "I'll give you a missed call." It doesn't work outside of India, though.

When I was small:

The rest of the English-speaking world says, "When I was young."

Timepass:

"What are you doing?" "Watching the pigeons." "Why?" "Just timepass." It's the action of spending time doing something that has no aim or is not very useful.

Expire:

In India, no one dies. Everyone expires.

At the rate of:

Jane from the US gives her email as, "jane at gmail dot com." But Ravi from Indore says, "ravi at the rate of gmail dot com." The @ symbol is spoken of in full.

Sit on his head:

"To get work done, I have to sit on his head" means I have to follow up with him frequently. It makes no sense anywhere else in the world.

Do the needful:

Do what's required. Even Britain doesn't use this outdated expression anymore.

Mugging:

We know it means memorisation or rote learning. To a non-Indian, it means stealing someone's money by threatening violence.

Aunty/Uncle:

This could be anyone unrelated who is older than you. I know a little boy who talks fondly of his favourite Bus Driver Uncle.

Any good news?:

This is asked of young women who got married the previous year. Since a straight "Are you pregnant?" is considered (rightly) brazen and indelicate, the workaround is a cheesy question while wearing a cheesy smile: "Any good news?" No foreigner is likely to understand this degree of nuance.

Do one thing:

This phrase, in practice, is often a request to do a list of things. "Do one thing. Call Didi and ask if she wants to join us. If she says no, call Anita Aunty and invite her. And if she says no, then..."

Under the strong and ever-present influence of our own mother tongue, we mould English in special ways that feel natural to us. Hence, some of us are likely to say something like: "Before me, there are two brothers, then is me, then two more sisters are coming."

Meaning: I have two elder brothers and two younger sisters.

*****

RSVP

So you get invited to a wedding. The invitation, whether online or offline, ends with an RSVP.

We all know the usage, of course. They are asking us to let them know if we're coming or not. Great.

RSVP. Répondez s'il vous plaît. Please reply.

It's like many other abbreviations we use in daily life: jpg, png, URL, http, SIM, PIN, OTP, KYC, RTO, MBBS, PhD, GPS, etc. Except RSVP is the only French one for some strange reason.

We use these abbreviations without much thinking. We know how and when to use them but don't always have a clue what the letters actually stand for. (What *is* jpg or MBBS?)

What we don't know, some of us invent.

Years ago, in his wisdom to make something of his son, my father sent me to attend Cost Accounting classes.

A lecturer in Corporate Law (or some such thing) suddenly asked if we'd ever noticed the RSVP inscription in wedding invitations.

Since the class was full of bespectacled geeks who had no life of their own or reluctant students like me who didn't engage, no one replied.

But the portly lecturer persisted. "I'm sure you must have noticed RSVP, right? OK. Do you know the full form of RSVP?"

There was a twinkle in his eye. "Many people think RSVP means Rasam, Sambar, Vada, Payasam." Affected deeply by his own witticism, his body spasmed with laughter. The geeks too thought it funny, a happy diversion from tax laws.

"Jokes apart, does anyone know the real answer? The full form of RSVP? Anyone?"

I could've put my hand up and given the answer but I didn't know how to pronounce the French words. How did you say répondez s'il vous plaît with all those horrible diacritical marks? I decided to shut up.

I waited for the lecturer to say it. I could learn something useful for the day. He did not disappoint. He had been building up to a punchline all this while. Now he let it fly like a loose cannon.

"It means," he said in ringing tones to reach the dullards in the back benches. "Refreshments Served Very Pleasantly."

The geeks nodded. The class went on. While I remember next to nothing about Corporate Law, I never forgot this novel literary invention.

You couldn't blame him. Who on earth decided to add a French term into our invitations? That is the person to blame.

*****

Why everything is awesome

How often do you say 'awesome'? Everyone does it all the time. Do we really think everything in life is awesome?

How did the meeting go? Awesome. You like the pickle? Awesome. Saw the match yesterday? Awesome.

It needn't even be an answer to a question. I got egg curry for lunch. Awesome. Today is my brother's birthday. Awesome.

In Facebook comments and WhatsApp messaging it's even reduced to 'osum.' Presumably to save significant energy while typing.

It used to originally mean 'inspiring awe.' No longer. It is now a casual assertion that says I heard you and I'm trying hard to show interest.

If you're younger, you say epic. How was lunch? Epic. We're going to Goa next week. Epic. I bought a DSLR. Epic.

In the literary world an epic refers to a grand account like Valmiki's *Ramayan*, Homer's *Iliad* or Tolstoy's *War and Peace*. For those who have actually read bits of such works, the everyday usage of 'epic' to refer to the quality of French fries at the local McDonald's takes some digesting.

It appears that we've always used offbeat, catch-all words.

To an earlier generation, the word was 'cool.' It was easily applied to anything that happened to anyone. It lacked the excess of 'awesome' and 'epic' and kept its emotional distance.

We used to live over there. Cool. How's your father now? Cool. I'm going to get a haircut. Cool.

In the 80's, the pop music world gave us a similar short-hand word: 'Groovy.'

How are you doing these days? Groovy. I got down from the bus and she smiled at me. Groovy. I took two wickets in two balls. Groovy.

In my college days, there was this guy, who, hailing from Calcutta, put an instinctive and memorable spin on the word. Gdoobee, he said. And for this innovation, forever enshrined, his name *became* Gdoobee. In all honesty, I do not remember his real name to this day.

So, it's not a new thing, after all. The catch-all word, in every generation, serves the same purposes. It's handy in any situation. It eliminates the need to think of a valid response. It's a ready answer when you don't know what to say. It makes it look like you care even when you don't. And it keeps the social wheels turning. You'll receive it as often as you dish it out.

With increasing regularity, the IPL final telecasts—even if disappointingly one-sided—attract a ginormous audience of 630 million people on Jio Hotstar alone.

Something like that, to my mind, is well and truly… awesome.

*****

What's an 'h' doing in Geetha?

The invitation reads Geetha weds Ranjith. If you wonder for a moment why there is an 'h' in the names, you must be a North Indian.

Say, the invitation reads Lata weds Tilak.

If you wonder for a moment why they didn't write 'Latha' and 'Thilak', you must be a South Indian.

The use of 'h', or not, in proper names reveals your origins.

An 'h' softens the sound of the 't' before it—as in math, not mat; cloth, not clot; thank, not tank; pithy, not pity; and so on. The hard 't' sound becomes the soft 't' sound.

We all know this instinctively—whoever speaks English, that is. To a South Indian, therefore, spelling it as 'Geetha' feels correct because the 't' sound is softened and ensures the name doesn't end up sounding like 'guitar' with the hard 't' sound. Logical, no-brainer. Right?

Not so fast.

If you're from North India, the 'h' has been fulfilling another function that is not at all about softening the 't' sound.

To you, the words 'kaali' and 'khaali', for instance, are entirely different.

The 'h' changes the meaning. It changes the sound. Black and empty. Two distinct words with two distinct sounds. The 'h' makes a difference. What's the confusion? It's so obvious.

Not so fast.

Most non-North Indians (in Coimbatore, Canberra or Coventry) pronounce the above words in much the same way. The 'h' makes no difference. Because, outside of North India, no one knows the 'rule' that 'h' is supposed to work as an aspirated consonant as well. They have no such sounds themselves.

Tushar, the North Indian, writes 'baari' (turn) and 'bhaari' (heavy) on the white board. Thejas, his South Indian pal, reads them out the same way. Tushar writes 'khaata' (accounts) and 'kaata' (bite). Thejas makes the same sound.

Tushar secretly wonders: what's wrong with these South Indians? Even the way Thejas spells his name is so weird.

Thejas secretly wonders: what's this crazy guy going on about? Shouldn't he spell his name Thushar to clarify the softened 't' sound, incidentally?

Who is right? North or South? To 'h' or not to 'h'?

It depends on whether you were born north or south of the Vindhyas. And how you bent English spelling to suit the sounds of your mother tongue if you came from the north.

Why let an 'h' divide us? The choices are either we stick to our regional guns or pause and think about where the other person is coming from.

If you've noticed, the invitation landscape is already changing for the better.

Mukti weds Santhosh. Preethi weds Gautam. Kavitha weds Pratap.

Hurrah to that.

* * * * *

9

English

Mondegreen

IF YOU'VE BEEN listening to rock music, you know it's often hard to make out the lyrics. They sing it their way and you hear it your way.

Jimi Hendrix famously sang the phrase "While I kiss the sky" which was heard by thousands as "While I kissed this guy."

CCR's popular song originally said, "There's a bad moon on the rise." Many heard it as "There's a bathroom on the right."

The great Beatles hit *Lucy in the Sky with Diamonds* had the line, "The girl with kaleidoscope eyes." Their die-hard fans heard it as, "The girl with colitis goes by."

Deep Purple's still-popular chorus (known for its timeless guitar riff) "Smoke on the water/Fire in the sky" was misheard as "Smoke on the water/Fire engine guy."

The lines from Nirvana's anthem *Smells like Teen Spirit* "Here we are now/Entertain us" were misheard as, "Here we are now/In containers."

There's actually a word for misheard lyrics like these:

Mondegreen.

Some mondegreens became so famous that artistes like Hendrix and CCR sang the misheard versions in their live concerts in a spirit of fun and tease.

It's not just in pop songs that mondegreens occur. The US national anthem begins with the lofty words, "Oh say, can you see, by the dawn's early light." Some heard them as "José, can you see…"

Mondegreens are not a modern phenomenon either. A line from an old Christian hymn "Gladly the cross I'd bear" was mistaken for "Gladly, the cross-eyed bear."

Occasionally, mondegreens had an interesting side-effect. Joe Cocker sang of a 'lovely planet' which was misheard as 'lonely planet.' The latter became the name of a well known travel guide series of books.

No one knows why we hear the wrong thing although there are theories. It's akin to the game of Chinese Whispers where the original line gets progressively distorted into some hilarious garbage by the time it reaches the last guy.

Mondegreens are not restricted to English alone. Growing up in the South, without any knowledge of Hindi, we were taught patriotic songs in Hindi by zealous teachers.

A popular one had the repeating phrase, "Bara tamata." We sang it with great gusto. Years later, some of us realised the actual words were "Bharat Mata."

'Mondegreen' sounds French but isn't. In 1954, a writer at Harper's Magazine remembered how as a little girl she misheard an old English ballad. The actual words, saluting a dead war hero, were:

They have slain the Earl o' Moray

And laid him on the green.

She heard them as:

They have slain the Earl o' Moray

And Lady Mondegreen.

And thus was born the word 'mondegreen' to signify all the misheard lyrics from that moment on.

Turns out mondegreen itself started life as a mondegreen.

* * * * *

Country phrases

Chinese whispers. Bermuda shorts. French toast. Country names in everyday phrases have strange and non-obvious origins.

French fries, for instance, are not French. They are Belgian. Deprived of fish from winter's frozen rivers, Belgians in the 1600s fried potato bits in fat instead.

Belgians consider that proof. The French don't. The rest of the world doesn't care. The US eats them as fries, the UK eats them as chips and India eats them—with added vividness—as finger chips.

What about French toast? The ancient Romans ate something called *aliter dulcia*—translated as 'another sweet dish'—which was bread soaked in milk and eggs and fried. More Latin than French.

A New York innkeeper in the 1700s made the same thing and called it French's toast to immortalise his own name, Joseph French. Unluckily for him, people ignored the apostrophe, as they always do, and reduced it to French toast. His loss, France's gain.

A Bermudian tea shop owner hemmed the trousers of his employees to keep them cool in the summer heat. The British Army, stationed there during World War I, loved the idea and shared it with the world as Bermudas.

Think of Sunil Gavaskar driving through the covers. Notice his trademark Panama hat. Wide brimmed, floppy and light. Does it come from Panama?

No, it's from Ecuador. The US president Theodore Roosevelt was photographed wearing one when the Panama Canal was being built. And the American public wasted no time in calling it a Panama hat.

Venetian blinds also block the sun but are not from Venice. They're not even from Italy. Either Egypt or Persia in the 1800s created them using reeds as slats.

Venetian merchants bought them, traded with the rest of the world and took the credit.

A pleasant period in someone's life or job is called an Indian summer. Given India's unbearable summer heat, that sounds off the mark, right?

The term refers to Native Americans from the 1700s and the unusually warm and enjoyable weather that sometimes occurs in the middle of autumn. It's nothing to do with the sweltering summers you and I know well.

England and Holland were sworn enemies in the 1600s. So English phrases with 'Dutch' in them are snide put-downs.

'Double Dutch' means gibberish. 'Dutch courage' means fake courage. 'To go Dutch' is where the man and woman share a dinner bill which to the Brits was crass and unchivalrous.

Surprisingly offensive is the origin of 'Chinese whispers', a game where a phrase is relayed in whispers and gets mangled to hilarious effect as it travels.

The origin is the Sinophobic idea of the 1800s that Chinese spoke in weird and unintelligible ways. In today's woke world, we'd call that attitude racist.

Mexican wave, Russian roulette, Siamese twins, Prussian blue, Singapore Sling, Greek tragedy... the list goes on.

An essay for another time, then.

*****

Irreversible binomials

Why do we say ladies and gentlemen, not gentlemen and ladies?

Why fish and chips, not chips and fish? Why give and take, not take and give?

Salt and pepper. Body and soul. Rich and famous. Wear and tear. Rock and roll. Cloak and dagger. Not the other way around. Why?

It's called idiomatic usage which means using words a certain way because that is the way they've been used before. Usage defined by custom. We do it like this because we did it like that.

It's like a child asking, "Why is the sky blue?" and you snapping, "It's like that only!" Idioms also are "like that only." No big reason. Just keep quiet.

So, it's cup and saucer, not saucer and cup. Cat and mouse, not mouse and cat. The order matters.

The formal term for these pairs of words in a specific order is irreversible binomials.

Irreversible because the order cannot be altered. And binomial because it's a pair of words (joined by a conjunction.) Say them together.

'Bells and whistles' is thus an irreversible binomial. As also yin and yang. Spick and span. Wine and dine. Tried and tested. You get the drift.

Now wear a superior air and greet someone at a party with, "Hi. I find irreversible binomials fascinating."

Chances are people will avoid your company. They will abruptly, in mid-conversation, wave to other folks and vacate your vicinity. No one loves those with big words and superior airs.

Leaving you to nurse your gin and tonic all alone. Notice it's gin and tonic, not tonic and gin. The order matters. If you down three of them rapidly, the order will not matter any more.

A looser definition of irreversible binomials includes phrases that use the same word twice: again and again, less and less, over and over, louder and louder, on and on, etc.

They are irreversible in the sense there's nothing to reverse. And binomial, they certainly are.

Remember, the word occurs *only* twice.

Let's say, after one too many, you stagger to the restroom, regurgitate into the commode and swear, "Never, never, never, never again." Four repeats and no conjunction.

However heart-felt, it's not an irreversible binomial. It falls in the category of You Are Drunk.

(This act of atoning in the loo, incidentally, is known as 'talking to God on the big white telephone' as Billy Connolly, the Scottish comedian, observed.)

Once you decide alcohol is bad, you drop the habit. And pick up the new habit of convincing others to stop drinking.

And passionately point out the error of their ways to your kith and kin. Not kin and kith, but kith and kin. (Kith are friends; kin are relatives.)

Irreversible binomials. Now that you know, go impress your near and dear. Not dear and near. The order matters.

*****

Words, old and new

Like old clothes, we discard old words. And try on new ones.

Negro, the Spanish word for black, was used freely by Martin Luther King in his 'I have a dream' speech. It later turned *coloured.* In the 90s, it became African American. Not good enough, said a writer:

I am not an African-American. I am an American. A proud Black American. Period. Don't cut my citizenry in half.

Fair point. So Black American it is for now.

A person unable to walk was lame. Shakespeare wrote, "They will not give a doit to relieve a lame beggar."

No longer. Your cat may be lame but not a human. We say 'lame excuse' and 'lame duck president' but that's about it. We don't apply it to a person who can't walk. Never mind the Bard. (A doit was a small sum of money, by the way.)

Language evolved. *Lame* became *cripple* and *cripple* became *handicapped*. In the 90s, it became *disabled*.

The French *derriere* became *arse* in British English and *ass* in US English. The crudeness was somewhat softened with *bum* (British) and *butt* (US).

William the Conqueror was also known as William the Bastard. It stated a fact without judgment. It wasn't the cuss word we hurl at a friend who drives our car too fast.

It comes from the French *batard* which also means, of all things, a type of bread, a short baguette. In English, a bastard title is a page with only the title of the book on it without the subtitle, author's name, edition, etc.

To get around this idea of irregularity, the UK uses *non-marital child*. Even better is *love child*, joyous and celebratory. It's the brand name of a cosmetics line today by Masaba. Bold and unabashed.

In the 1920s, psychiatrists used terms that sound shocking to us today: 'imbeciles' had IQs between 25 and 50, 'idiots' were below 25, and 'morons' ranged from 51 to 70. We cannot even believe they were purely clinical terms. Today we say *intellectually challenged* along with a host of well considered words.

A harmless word facing extinction was *pregnant*. It wasn't used in polite conversation. Preferred alternatives: 'She is with child.' 'She is expecting.' 'She is in the family way.' '*Khush khabri hai?*' The US even banned *pregnant* on TV in the 50s.

Presumably, the reason was that it implied the parents had had sex and this information could corrupt the youth of America. Lucille Ball, the mega star of the TV show *I Love Lucy*—in a delicious irony—became pregnant in real life during the second season. It was believed sex had something to do with it.

There's a pattern here.

It starts with a word, squeaky clean. Someone uses it as a slur. Many follow. The word feels awkward. We seek a safer word.

Till someone uses it as a slur…

And on it goes.

*****

Caught between the US and the UK

Which is correct? Coriander or cilantro? Chips or crisps?

We follow British English because they ruled us. We follow American English because the whole world does so. And we get pulled this way and that.

Lay's Chips introduced cilantro as a flavour. "Cool," we said, until we realised it was US English for the common coriander.

What's inside a Lay's pack? Chips, say Indians and Americans. Crisps, say the British. When Brits say chips, they mean what the world calls French fries and Indians call finger chips.

Brits and Indians say *sweets* to refer to the boiled concoctions of yesteryear, Nutrine and today's Parle as well as the unbranded crescent shapes in orange and yellow.

Americans call all that *candy*, not sweets. The only time Brits say candy is when they buy the pink, airy, wispy thing on a stick at a village fair. They call it candy floss. Americans call it cotton candy. Indians say either, depending on what your teachers taught you.

Talking of fairs, what we call a giant wheel is a Ferris Wheel in the US. And has no specific name in the UK. (Barring the famous, humongous one for visitors called the London Eye.)

The frozen fruity thing on a stick—the UK calls it an ice lolly. The US calls it a popsicle. We call it an ice cream even though it only has ice and no cream.

Brown & Polson introduced us to a wobbly gelatine dessert called jelly. But the Americans call the same thing Jell-O (after a brand name). They can't call it jelly because they say jelly to indicate the thing we and the Brits call jam. Yes, our jam is their jelly. And our jelly is their Jell-O. Clear?

The US used to say *carry out* for food packed in a restaurant and eaten elsewhere. The Brits say *take away*. The US now says *take out*. In India, in places like McDonald's, you'll mostly hear *take away*. However, to take *idli*-chutney home from an Udupi restaurant, you'd do well to use our very own *parcel*.

Sometimes, the differences are tiny and subtle. What the US calls *corn*, the UK calls s*weet corn*. What the US calls *skim milk*, the UK uses the more grammatical *skimmed milk*. Similarly, it's *sour cream* in the US but *soured cream* in the UK.

Perhaps, the strangest one is what the US calls an eggplant, the purple vegetable that looks like an egg (sometimes). The Brits call it aubergine from the French, which makes the humble veggie sound posh. Indians call it neither. We have our own name for it… brinjal.

How did that happen?

Brinjal originates from the Portuguese word *beringela*, which itself came from the Arabic *badinjan*. The Arabs got it from the neighbouring Persians, who called it *badingan*. And, in turn, the Persians got it from the Sanskrit *vatingana*. The linguistic journey of the vegetable began in India, went to the West and returned with a foreign accent as a brinjal.

Like people, words travel. And return home with interesting tales to tell.

*****

To hyphenate or not

When do you combine two words as one? Is it web site or website? Is it login or log in? Is it proof reader or proofreader? Or, with a hyphen, proof-reader?

It's fascinating that many compound words in English began life as separate words. Centuries ago, the present time was referred to as 'to day' which became 'to-day' for a few hundred years. And, of course, we know it as 'today' in the present times.

Because the 'e' stood for 'electronic,' the British decided to preserve its origin and hyphenated 'e-mail'. The Americans, pragmatic and cavalier as ever, dropped the hyphen and wrote 'email.'

In recent times, the British too began to drop the hyphen. It's safe to say 'email' is the preferred form. You don't capitalise the first letter (Email) either—unless, of course, it's the first word in a sentence. Many words follow this pattern: open spelling as two words at first, followed by its hyphenated compound form and ending up with closed spelling as one word.

Proof reader. Proof-reader. Proofreader.

On line. On-line. Online.

Web site. Web-site. Website.

If you go to a US bank site, say Citibank, you'll see 'Login' and 'Logout' as single closed spelling words.

But at a Brit bank site, say HSBC, you'll see 'Log on' and 'Log off'. Not only is it open spelling as two words but, as a bonus, the second words are 'on' and 'off' instead of 'in' and 'out.'

Some words never make it to the third stage. They stop at the hyphenated version.

H-bomb, T-shirt, U-turn, X-ray.

(These words always begin with a capital even in the middle of a sentence.)

But don't push it. Don't apply this 3-part rule indiscriminately. Don't make single words on a whim. Not in professional writing.

'At least' is still two words. You don't write 'atleast', as some folks do. 'In fact' is still two words. Not 'infact.'

'Up to' is still two words. Not 'upto.' (Just because it resembles 'into' and 'onto' which are single words.)

So, is your head going into a tail spin now? Or is it going into a tail-spin? Or is it going into a tailspin? Full marks if your head went with the third choice.

All of this matters, deliciously so, if you are a professional writer or aspire to be one. Others will find their own fun ways to feel awesome.

They might even spell it as 'osum.'

*****

Retronyms

If you're a certain age, you once knew an unmovable desktop thing that rang in offices and homes. You called it a phone.

Today a phone means a mobile phone. The old desktop thing is no longer a phone. It goes by a new name: a landline.

Yesterday's textbooks called the orbiting moon a satellite. After Russia shot up Sputnik to also orbit the earth, textbooks looked at the moon in a new light. It's a *natural* satellite, they noted, revising their opinion.

A guitar was a guitar for centuries. Then came the electric guitar. And the old instrument suddenly morphed into an *acoustic* guitar.

It happens all the time. With every forward step, old things get renamed.

Such names have a name.

Retronyms.

Long ago, my neighbours were the first ones on our street to get a TV. Their pride was punctured when, in the fullness of time, later technology renamed their possession from a TV to a *black and white TV*.

When cameras turned digital, the older ones were renamed as *film* cameras. When jet engines were affixed, older airplanes became *propeller* airplanes.

When ovens turned microwave and wars turned nuclear, the older versions became conventional ovens and conventional wars.

Chocolate was originally a drink before it became a slab. Once the sweet slabs and bars got popular, what happened to the drink? It got renamed as *hot chocolate*.

For something to be a car, it needed an engine, wheels, a steering, a gear box and so on. Someone invented a gearbox that worked automatically. We rushed to find a retronym for the old car: 'manual transmission' sounded perfect.

If what Apple makes is a watch, what was the thing that HMT once made? An *analog* watch.

People who lived through the First World War didn't call it that. They couldn't have known there would be a second one later on. They called it the Great War. When Hitler pulled his global stunt later on, he forced us to invent a retronym for the earlier war.

Mail means email. Not what a flesh-and-blood postman has delivered at your home for decades. That old thing has a new name: snail mail. Try telling your grandpop.

For centuries, milk meant milk from mammals. With the advent of cocoa milk, almond milk and other plant-based milk, we resorted to a retronym for good old regular milk: *dairy* milk.

Thus far, human relationships have escaped retronyms. No technology has invented new relationships to replace old ones. Therefore, a mother is still a mother. A cousin is still a cousin. (In Indian English, we do talk of a *real* brother, though.).

The recent LGBTQ movement has forced us to find a retronym for the majority who are not in any of these categories: *straight.*

Retronyms. They redefine what happened before.

Think of them as a backward glance at the past as we hurtle towards an ever-inventive future.

*****

Animal phrases

We often use everyday English phrases that feature animals. We talk of 'the elephant in the room' or of someone who 'gets my goat.'

Where do these strange phrases come from?

A less worthy member among our relatives is called the black sheep of the family. In farming counties like Derbyshire and Kent, a rare black sheep among the regulars was once actually considered lucky.

At some point, the tide turned. 'Black sheep' became someone not like others and of lesser worth. A black sheep's wool fetched lower prices because it could not be dyed. For that reason, your differently talented uncle is a black sheep today.

To get someone's goat is to annoy someone. This comes from race horses. Like people, horses too feel lonely. Horse owners placed goats in stables to help them relax.

Wily competitors removed the goats to spook the horse and make it lose the race. Annoying, right?

Another from the equine world: straight from the horse's mouth. Sellers of horses, like car dealers of today, embellished facts to make a sale.

A savvy buyer directly looked into the animal's mouth and gauged its teeth to find out its true age. Truth revealed. Straight from the horse's mouth.

The elephant in the room is the issue in plain sight but we avoid discussing it because it's awkward or difficult. This picturesque phrase comes from the Russian writer Ivan Krylov who wrote a story of a man who noticed all the trinkets in a museum but missed the elephant.

Dostoevsky popularised the phrase by talking of a character in his own work being "just like Krylov's Inquisitive Man who didn't notice the elephant in the museum."

On a hot summer day, you say you are sweating like a pig. But do pigs sweat? Not really. Then how come? In the smelting industry, the original phrase was 'sweating like pig iron.' When hot pig iron is poured on sand, it cools and solidifies into tiny droplets, much like sweat.

Someone down the line dropped the 'iron' and forever ruined the non-sweaty reputation of pigs.

Hunting dogs, especially the old ones, often barked at wrong locations that held no prey. So, when someone is barking up the wrong tree—pursuing a mistaken line of thought or action—he or she is mimicking an old dog barking up a wrong tree looking for prey that isn't there.

My own favourite is 'raining cats and dogs.' How on earth did that come about? In Britain of the 1500's, the thatched roofs on houses were of straw piled up in layers without solid wood underneath. Little dogs and cats huddled in the straw for warmth.

In heavy rain, some of them got washed off and slid into the gutters below. And the people described the heavy rain, "Oh, my. It's raining cats and dogs." You couldn't blame them. They were only reporting what they saw.

So be kind to animals. They add colour to your speech.

*****

Clarity

When you begin your writing journey, you observe good writers. People who seem to know what they're doing. Whether authors, content writers or copywriters.

You are curious, ambitious, willing to learn. Which is a good thing at any age. You are prepared to work hard. Which is a great thing at any age.

You have a deep love for language. Which is a... problem at any age. A writer falling in love with words is only natural but has its pitfalls.

Suddenly, you want to make your work interesting instead of clear. You want to include every neat little wordplay, every corner-of-the-eye observation, every oddball idea that suggests itself. You are seduced by decoration, not substance.

You allow little ideas pull you away from your main line of thought, which is what a piece of good writing is.

You will not be the first writer in the world to be sucked in by the need to be clever rather than clear.

Clarity.

It's the holy grail in writing. Everything else is side show. If you have nothing to say, you may as well not say it. Instead of clothing it with vagueness and hoping someone somewhere will get something out of it. They won't.

Clarity.

All your favourite authors wrote many drafts to ensure crystal-clear communication. It is a courtesy you owe your reader. You are telling him or her that you've put in the work so they'll find it easy. Not the other way around.

Clarity.

Never assume you have it in your writing. Effective writing only appears simple. It never is.

You have to work for it, whether it's a film script or a social media post. To be outside of your writing and look at your words as though written by someone else is a hard-won but basic skill. Write and rewrite—till the meaning jumps out.

Trust me, I can hear you yell: Isn't clarity boring? You want me to be PowerPoint? You want me to be Wikipedia?

What about all the colourful, entertaining and spontaneous flimflam I want to bring along to my writing to give it some piss and vinegar?

Here's the trick. Use any ornamentation you want. Restraint is the key. Don't avoid, but don't overindulge either.

If you express every incidental thought that comes into your head, we know you are an enthusiastic amateur. If you stay on track, we recognise a real writer.

We have all listened to a presenter in a hall who meandered along in the belief that they were far more entertaining or humorous than they actually were.

Don't be that guy.

Even a non-professional writer, writing to express or share, needs to answer only a single question: Am I being clear? Answer it, don't assume it. All else will follow in time.

Hopefully, this satisfies all those people who asked me for writing tips. About four of them at last count.

* * * * *

The way to end

It's called a valediction. The way you close a letter or email. As a mark of appreciation, you could end your email with 'Thanks' or 'Many thanks' or a simple 'Thank you.'

You could have a professional closing with 'Best regards' or 'Warm regards' or, even simply, 'Best.'

If you wish to be formal to someone in power or is senior to you, you write 'Respectfully', 'Sincerely' or 'Sincerely yours.'

To close in a friendly manner, you write 'Cheers', 'All my best' or 'Keep in touch.'

Like with any form of writing, valedictions give a clue to the mood of the writer.

If you use a plain and simple 'Best' as part of your signature, that is a decision to be neutral and nonintrusive.

If someone you just got to know moves from 'Yours sincerely' to 'Best regards' to 'Cheers' inside of a week, you must be doing something right. They are obviously warming up to you.

Valedictions, of course, come from the earlier world of hand-written letters and formal relationships. Thanks to the British civil service, the phrase 'I remain, Sir, your most humble and obedient servant' was a familiar closing.

An arrogant and irreverent (though loveable) character like Samuel Johnson wrote this in closing to a Lord Chesterfield: 'Your lordship's most humble, most obedient servant, Samuel Johnson.' It was a formality. Not a sucking up.

According to royal etiquette today, if you are a government boffin in the UK writing to King Charles, you are expected to close with 'Your Royal Highness's most humble and obedient servant. Regards.'

All this business about servility and obedience of the 18th century got abbreviated to 'Yours faithfully' in later times. And, as a less boot-licking variation, 'Yours sincerely.'

In today's world of haste, emojis and who-cares-for-niceties aggression, there is no place for even implied subservience.

That is why the neutral 'Best' is popular. It says very little, asks for nothing much and merely marks the ending of an e-mail.

In the early days of e-mail, we had homilies that expressed a moral or a lofty thought. A clever signature line, you hoped, put out a pretty picture of your soul.

I myself used something I'd read somewhere as a signature 'It's all good in the end. If it's not good, it's not the end.'

Wacky signatures are common today. Like, 'Stay luminous, stay hydrated.'

It's good to spend a few seconds on valedictions. It makes you interesting. It's fun. It says you're not bland, you have character.

You can vary it in different emails to the same person depending on the mood you want to convey.

'Peace out.' 'Stay classy.' 'Live, laugh, love.' 'Catch up.' 'Thanks for your time.' 'Tree hugs.' 'Until next time.' 'Lukewarm regards.'

It's a small thing, of course. But it can be a *nice* small thing.

Cheers.

* * * *

About the Author

Narayan Kumar is a seasoned copywriter with over 35 years of experience in leading ad agencies of India. He is an independent branding consultant and website builder and writes a weekly post on LinkedIn on all things Indian from subjects as varied as social mores and quirks, rural towns, workplace anecdotes and the fascinating twists and turns of Indian English. He spends his time between Mumbai and his second home in the Nilgiri hills.

Narayan Kumar

Wadala East, Mumbai

www.bluemountaincode.com

www.triptychnilgiris.com

narayan@bluemountaincode.com